Headless

A MERGED WORLDS NOVELLA

SAMANTHA MARSHALL

STARDUST
EMPIRE
PUBLISHING

In the Beginning...

This novella originally appeared in the anthology *A Perfectly Paranormal Halloween*, released in October, 2021.

This amazing anthology is well worth a read - apart from Headless, there are three other amazing stories to gorge on!

Check it out here:
https://books2read.com/u/3n29xK

GLOSSARY OF TERMS

Want to know more about a specific character? You've come to the right place!

I keep a working Character Glossary for each of my worlds on my website.

Check it out here:

www.sliceofsammy.com/character-glossary/

To Disney's Halloween Feast, which first introduced me to the concept of the Headless Horseman.

To the Monster Mash, and the Time Warp, upon which my love of both fun and spooky are built.

To Big Boo's Haunt, where I learned to love cute little ghosts with their tongues hanging out, and to Mad Monster Mansion, where I laughed every time I got turned into a pumpkin and flushed down the toilet.

To Terry Pratchett, who had me falling head over heels for Death the first time I ever read him, and is consequently responsible for my fascination with skellingtons.

To Link, who taught me that monsters disappear when the sun comes up, and that it's okay to put ghosts in a bottle until you're ready to face them.

To the Scarlet Monastery Graveyard, which I visited every year without fail and still managed to never get hold of the elusive flying horse. To Shtinky, who got the horse first try and rode it everywhere for the next fifteen years with a smug look on his face.

To Illidan, who taught me that demons could be sexy.

To the friends who have never questioned my penchant for drawing ghosts, reading vampire books, howling at the moon and just generally being kooky.

To everyone, everywhere, who loves a bit of Halloween aesthetic all year round, just like I do.

Most of all, to those beyond the veil. I hear you.
♥

BEGIN AS YOU MEAN TO GO ON

Trees loomed ahead, and Devlin's fingers tightened on the wheel as the RV bumped off the road and onto the grass. Despite reading the operations manual from cover to cover several times, in the heat of the moment he couldn't remember which of the various pedals was for acceleration, braking or, in a twist of creative inspiration he'd never understand, the built-in drinking spout which jettisoned water in case of an unreasonable thirst.

He stomped down hard with his left foot and yelped as said water splashed across his chest. Not that one, clearly – and those evergreens really did look quite menacing, now that he was close enough to make out individual branches. Shifting his foot to the right, Devlin stomped again and the RV jerked to a halt, momentum throwing him against the dish-like centre of the steering wheel hard enough to set the horn blaring – a sound that cut off as the vehicle rocked back on its axle, returning his body to the seat amidst a symphony of clanging pots, clattering crockery and Bailey's indignant shriek.

"My pardon," he called, offering a sheepish grin. Bailey glared from where she now lay upside down on the floor after tumbling off the RV's bed, blankets tangled around her legs.

1

Devlin sighed, pushing himself upright. "Stopping is more complicated than it at first appears."

Bailey curled a lip.

"Are you injured?" Devlin tried to peer down the length of the vehicle, but his head had lodged at an awkward angle on the dash. When Bailey didn't answer, he braced against the steering wheel and leaned over until he could tangle his fingers in his own hair. Ignoring the sharp tug against his scalp, he positioned his head under one arm and levered out of the driver's seat.

Perusing one's environment from one's own armpit had taken some getting used to – and a revised hygiene routine – but after more centuries than he dared record, Devlin had become accustomed to it. He'd become accustomed to a lot of things, the sort of things he'd never imagined having to become accustomed to until his head was permanently separated from his body. Such was the nature of being cursed.

"Hold still a moment, or you'll make it worse." Devlin sat his head on a stack of books so that he could see both his body and Bailey, then set about disentangling her legs from the blanket and getting her back onto the bed without either of them tripping over one another. That trick alone had taken him decades to perfect – though perfection, really, was in the eye of the beholder, and Bailey wasn't the kind to be impressed when one poked her in said eye because he'd placed his head at a strange angle and couldn't quite see her face.

He took a half step back from the bed. "Better now?"

Bailey narrowed her eyes at him.

"I'll take that as a yes. Will you accompany me on my errand, or am I going alone?"

Her eyes narrowed further, until her irises were little more than baleful slits.

"Alone it is." Devlin straightened the clothes he'd obtained at their previous rest stop.

He was still becoming used to modern clothing, but the tight denim he'd acquired felt somewhat, if not exactly, like his old leather breeches and the black t-shirt, though a little snug, was reminiscent of the linen shirts he'd once worn beneath his tunic. Since the shop owners had screamed and fled when he'd accidentally knocked his head off on a low-hanging display, Devlin hadn't been able to ask about armour or even pay for his items – but he'd found a stand of leather jackets that, whilst their protective value appeared doubtful, were lined with fleece and had a nice, high collar.

Devlin picked up the roll of flexible, adhesive cloth he'd discovered in the RV's bathing room and examined the box. "This ... kinesio-tape claims maximum adhesion with minimal skin irritation, and yet my head still fell off. Maybe I didn't use enough?"

Bailey rolled over to stare at the wall.

"I apologised for the sudden stop," Devlin grumbled, pulling the roll of tape from the box. It was a brilliant lime green with a removable backing protecting the sticky side. "I cannot do this alone, Bailey. Please."

She heaved a dramatic sigh, then shuffled to the edge of the bed and picked his head up by the hair. While Devlin faced the mirrored closet door, Bailey held his head on top of his neck so that he could secure it in place with the tape.

"Is it on straight?"

Bailey eyed him up and down, then jerked her chin in a nod and returned to the bed.

"Are you going to cease talking to me for the rest of the day?" Devlin snipped off several long lengths of tape and began wrapping the stuff around his neck as best he could. When he had a band as wide as his four fingers, he stopped and jumped up and down in place. "I'm far more hopeful about this excessive amount of tape. My head feels almost solid."

Bailey grunted, but some of the tension eased from her shoulders.

"Do you think I should take my sword?" Devlin twisted to look out of one of the RV's windows, eyeing the township beyond. Nobody in this new, modern world carried swords and the few times he'd tried, he'd had a less than ideal reception. He clicked his tongue against his teeth. "No sword."

Bailey sniggered.

"I fail to see the joke," Devlin snapped, snatching his leather jacket from the hook on the back of the door. "You're not the one facing a journey without her sword strapped in place atop her armour."

He drew his jacket on, then picked up a striped black and grey scarf and wound it around his neck to hide the tape. Tucking the ends of the scarf into themselves, Devlin fastened the jacket via the unusual but convenient contraption he'd learned was called a zipper, and held his arms out for inspection.

"Well?"

Bailey's eyes drifted unerringly to his hair, long enough that one of them could grab it in order to carry his head around. At the current moment, it stuck up at all angles, testament to the fact that they'd both been doing exactly that.

"Not much I can do," Devlin muttered, trying to fix the unruly mess as best he could. "If I comb it, I run the risk of dislodging my head entirely."

Bailey's lips pressed together but laughter shone in her eyes. Devlin grumbled as he stomped back to the front of the RV, snatching the silver key from the ignition and sliding it into his pocket.

"Defend our home then, if you're not coming along." Without bothering to wait for her answer, he opened the door and climbed down to the ground.

A chill wind swept the grassed area in which he'd parked the vehicle, swirling dust and leaves before it. Devlin was glad of his scarf and jacket as he closed the door of the RV and made his way towards the small cluster of shops on the other side of the road. Clouds hung overhead, dark with the threat of rain, and the early morning saw a thin fog curling against the ground much like a lazy cat.

He risked a glance down at his palms, still bearing the same callouses they had at the moment of his ... not quite death. Broad hands, flecked with scars he'd earned honourably – or at least, that's what he'd thought at the time. Devlin clenched his hands and shoved them in his jacket pockets. His neck itched the further he went and every curious face that turned his way made him flinch – but nobody screamed or backed away as he rounded the front of the nearest building, following the phantom tug in his chest that had led him on such a wild chase.

The shops were clumped together in groups of two or three, with neatly swept front steps and coloured awnings. Gut twisting, Devlin hesitated outside a shop with stylised letters on the door and magical paraphernalia in the windows. If he were to progress further, to reach for the one and only thing that could absolve his many sins, he would have to confront a creature he'd once sworn to hunt and destroy; a creature to whom he now owed a terrible debt.

Shame burnt his cheeks as he studied the shiny brass handle before him. Had he really come so far only to balk now? He thought of all the long, lonely years he and Bailey had been trapped in their secluded hollow and frowned. He owed it to her, to his sins, and to himself to set things right once and for all – to have courage, even in the darkest times.

Squaring his shoulders, Devlin opened the door and went in search of a demon.

MIND YOUR MANNERS

TUCKED IN A CHAIR by the open fire, Ivory hummed softly to herself as she ground pestle into mortar. It was well past the time she usually lingered at Mystic Madhouse, and she certainly wasn't of a mind to turn the raw materials she sold into actual products, but ... with Halloween only a few days away, the little shop was overrun with requests for outlandish ingredients and pre-brewed potions. Jacinta had reached out for help and though Ivory didn't much like being beholden to anyone, she did owe the businesswoman a favour or two.

Ivory glanced over the meticulously detailed potion recipe on the arm of the chair and then down at her mortar and pestle, judging the state of the ingredients inside. Being what she was, she didn't need the recipe for more than the list of components – nor did she require the ridiculous verse the author insisted must be chanted while the mixture was formalised into a whole.

Dipping a clawed finger into the mortar, Ivory drew out the tiniest sample of her work and flicked it into the open fire. A great hiss went up, as though some horrid beast crouched among the logs, and the flames flared momentarily blue before returning to their normal orange and yellow.

Perfect.

"Um ... Ivory?"

Swallowing a sigh, Ivory glanced towards the doorway where Jacinta stood wringing her hands. "What is it?"

"There's a ... uh. Someone here, that I ... um. I need your help."

"*My* help?" Ivory tipped her head to the side, brow furrowing. Jacinta was a powerful mage, the left forearm bared by her sleeveless dress marked by two thick bands of sapphire blue that warned anyone who cared to look that she was well and truly capable of defending herself. "What for?"

"It's ..." Jacinta trailed off, pinching the bridge of her nose. "You'll see. Please?"

Please. Ack. Ivory made a face, the very air souring with the taste of such a pathetic word. Still, Jacinta had opened Mystic Madhouse to her when she was starving. When nobody else would so much as twitch aside their blinds, the mage had offered kindness and acceptance – a gift Ivory had snatched with greedy hands, even as she hated herself for needing it.

"Fine," Ivory groused, rolling out of her chair. After a final grind of mortar against pestle, she tipped the mixture into a jar, screwed on the lid and dusted her hands together. "I can finish the liniment later."

Jacinta's gaze tracked to the recipe balanced on the arm of Ivory's chair. "I thought it was a draught?"

"A liniment will work better."

"The recipe says—"

"The recipe is stupid," Ivory snapped. "As is whoever wrote it. Were they watching old cartoons about witches while they squiggled in their fake pigskin notebook?"

Jacinta rolled her eyes. "You really are a bitch, you know that?"

"Thank you." Ivory followed the other woman out the door and down the short flight of stairs to the main shop. "Are you sure want me going out there? Looking like *this*?"

"I need you to," Jacinta said, her expression sombre in a way Ivory had rarely seen. "Pl—"

"Don't say it," Ivory snapped. She dusted her hands on her jeans, then blew out a breath. "Fine. You were warned."

Mystic Madhouse was set out much like a conventional grocery store, with neat aisles running parallel down the length of the floor. The sales counter was at the back of the area, blocking access to the rest of the building, and the glass windows at the opposite end let in enough light to see by without blinding. For the most part, the shop was functional more than ornamental – but with Halloween only a matter of days away, jack o'lanterns dotted every available surface while cheerful bats and smiling skeletons peered down from the evergreen garlands framing the walls and windows.

A man stood at the counter, his eyes a peculiar shade of light green that was anything but natural. Long lashes lowered to half-mast as he turned those eyes on her, giving him an air of menace that immediately piqued Ivory's interest. He was almost obscenely tall, with shoulders broad enough to block out most of the light from the windows. Though shadows clung to his form, they were no impediment to Ivory's vision; she drank in the rugged lines of his face, from his shaggy, dark brown hair to the slight scruff on his jaw and the tiny scar that bisected the skin just below his left eye. A striped scarf poked from the high collar of a black leather jacket, below which Ivory glimpsed jeans that fit tight enough to show off unfairly muscular thighs.

Handsome wasn't a strong enough word to describe him – in fact, if she'd been the poetic type, Ivory fancied there wouldn't *be* a word to accurately portray the look of him correctly. If that wasn't bad enough, he opened his mouth and the words that poured out were guttural and deep, the intonation in his voice striking against Ivory's soul as though she were some ritual instrument he alone knew how to play. Her breath caught as the sounds rolled over her, *through* her, and when he stopped, she could only turn to Jacinta and gape.

The mage spread her hands and shrugged. "I have no idea what he's saying. Do you?"

Ivory swallowed, and when she turned back to the man, found him eyeing her as intensely as she'd been eyeing him. She lifted a hand to the black horns that curled from her skull just behind her temples, somewhat reminiscent of a ram's but much, much deadlier. Even after all these years, instinct screamed at her to cover them, but instead, she tugged one of her black dread-locks and tried to recall how Jacinta addressed her customers.

"May I help you?" Ivory offered, speaking in the same language he'd used.

The man frowned, looking for all the world as though he'd bitten into a sour lemon. "I come seeking a demon."

Ivory snorted. "There's only one kind of man who goes looking for demons – and if you're going to try and murder me in this store, Hunter, it'll be the last mistake you ever make."

"You misunderstand. I am no Hunter," he replied, the gravel in his voice rasping over her skin until Ivory fought the urge to shiver. "You, however, appear to be a demon."

"What gave it away? The horns, or the claws? The black eyes, perhaps? Or maybe ..." Ivory drew her lips wide in the parody of a smile. "The fangs?"

The stranger touched a scarred hand to his breastbone. "I know because I can feel it."

Ivory took a second look at the way those pale green eyes seemed to flicker with their own internal light and felt her heart skip a beat. "You're a demon, too."

The man jerked backwards as though slapped, making a swift grab for his head. When he lowered his hands a moment later, his expression was so conflicted that Ivory let out a dreamy sounding sigh. He was so full of angst, so gorgeous and tortured, and it was *perfect*.

"I was not always a demon," he muttered. "I was cursed by one, and I deserved it. For eons, I've endured my punishment without complaint but now ... now that I'm free to travel the

9

Earth, I wish to atone for my sins." Drawing himself up to his full height, he pinned Ivory with those bright eyes. "In order to repent, I need the curse broken – and my quest has brought me here."

An ancient demon, a curse, and a quest? Ivory snorted. If the guy in front of her wasn't so clearly brimming with demonic energy, she'd have laughed him out of the store and then kicked his ass all the way down the street.

"What does he want?" Jacinta hissed from behind the counter.

Ivory switched languages, darting a glance at her employer. "To have a curse broken."

"A curse?" Jacinta raised an eyebrow. "I could take a look, I suppose—"

"A demonic curse."

"Oh." She shrugged. "Nothing I can do about that."

"I know." Turning back to the towering stranger, Ivory spoke in his language again. "Jacinta can't help you. Her magic is strong, but not in the way you need."

He frowned. "Unless you're the one named Jacinta, then it is not her help I'm seeking."

"Me?" Ivory took a half step back, then laughed. "Wait, wait, wait. You think *I* can break your curse?"

"You must." Bracing both enormous hands on the counter, the man leaned forward. "Though we've never met, the tug of my curse does not lie. You are the one, the descendant of she who bound me." His fingers curled, as though he might sprout claws and dig them into the wood but, to Ivory's disappointment, nothing happened. "It is you and you alone who can break the spell and allow my debt to be repaid. Please."

Ivory curled her lip. Please, this. Please, that. It was what everyone said to get what they wanted – but the moment they had it? She was little more than a novelty whose shine had worn off, revealing the monster underneath. Gods, she hated that word.

"Not in the shop!" Jacinta yelped, tugging at Ivory's sleeve for attention. "It took me forever to fix the damage last time."

"What?" Ivory blinked at the mage, then belatedly realised she'd bared her teeth on a threatening hiss. Forcing her body to relax, she shook her head. "Don't worry; I won't break anything."

The man's gaze lit on Jacinta's smattering of freckles and neatly styled brown hair, and his expression softened. "Peace. As soon as your colleague and I reach an arrangement, I'll be gone and you'll be free to go about your business."

"She doesn't understand you," Ivory growled. "You have to speak English."

He blinked. "Am I not?"

"No." Ivory rounded the corner of the desk, ignoring Jacinta's pleas for them to take the situation outside. "You're speaking demonic."

Astonishment blanked his features before those lashes once again lowered to half mast. "Well, that explains a great many things. Perhaps when you break the—"

"No," Ivory repeated, moving forward until the toes of her shoes bumped his boots. "Find someone else to break your curse; someone who doesn't mind being ordered around."

"Ordered? I asked," he protested, holding both hands up in placation. "I spoke from the heart."

Ew. Ew, ew, ew. Ivory set a hand against his glorious chest and shoved until the stranger backed up several steps. "For the last time, no. Now get out of this shop, or I will throw you out."

Surprise and hurt shifted quickly to anger, those bright eyes snapping with demonic fire. "I should like to see you try."

Laughter bubbled in Ivory's chest and she darted closer, swiping out with clawed fingers. In a move so swift it was a blur, he wrapped a hand around her wrist and twisted. She went with the motion, leaping onto the counter and cartwheeling through the air to land on the opposite side. The stranger released her wrist with a grunt and she smacked his arm aside. With a sharp twist of her body, Ivory curled her free hand in his jacket and tucked one foot behind his ankle.

Jacinta screamed. Remembering that she wasn't supposed to damage the shop, Ivory resisted the urge to toss him over her shoulder and instead swept the man's foot out from beneath him, dumping him flat on his back at her feet. He hit the floorboards hard enough to shake the entire building, but it wasn't the unusually heavy impact that took Ivory's attention – it was the moment his head detached from his shoulders, rolling across the floor to lodge against a rack of tarot cards like some macabre sort of bowling ball.

"Damn," said the head. "I should have used more tape."

Jacinta screamed again, only this time it was a very different sort of scream; one that wasn't in warning but in anger. Glass tinkled, magic crackled in the air and before Ivory had a chance to so much as blink, the front of the shop exploded.

TAINTED AT BEST

IF DEVLIN WAS HONEST with himself – and after thousands upon thousands of years with only Bailey for company, there was no reason to lie – he hadn't been prepared to come face to face with the creature he'd sought for so long and find her ... beautiful.

Gorgeous.

Bearing the sort of face greater men than he would compose ballads about, and the sort of body that those greater men would have wept into their ale over. And since he was far, far removed from those greater men, Devlin had even found her demonic attributes attractive, wondering what it'd be like to run his hands over her horns or feel her sharp teeth grazing his skin.

Clearly, he was depraved.

Maybe even insane.

Probably both, since what he thought had been a respectable speech had sent her into a rage. And now, here he was, his head jammed most embarrassingly underneath a shelf, able to do little more than watch while his body was picked up by the force of the explosion and tossed against the shop counter, flattening the demon in the process.

"Jacinta?" The demon shoved his body aside and dragged herself upright. "Jacinta!"

Coughing preceded the mage, chest heaving as she staggered from the back room. "I'm fine. The shield spell won't hold long, so – holy shit!"

Devlin grimaced as the mage's eyes locked on his stump of a neck. The demon, too, seemed transfixed as he stood and dusted himself off before reaching to dislodge his head from beneath the shelf.

"Is he ... is that ..." The mage shook her head as though to clear it, her face turning green, then white, then green again.

"It's all right," Devlin muttered, tugging the remains of the kinesio-tape from his skin. "I won't hurt you."

The mage lifted her hands and swallowed. "Ivory?"

"He says he won't hurt you," the demon – Ivory – said, peering around Devlin to look towards the front of the shop. "And right now, he's the least of our worries. There are Demon Hunters out there."

"Hunters?" Jacinta frowned. "I haven't said anything, I swear."

"I know." Ivory hissed out a breath. "Either they've picked up my trail some other way ... or they're here for him."

"Me?" Devlin frowned. "It's possible. I had a few, er, unusual occurrences on my way here that may have drawn undue attention."

Ivory raised a sculpted brow. "I can't imagine why."

"Yes. Well." Devlin tucked his head under one arm and tried not to pout. "Keeping my head on top of my shoulders is more difficult than it sounds."

Ivory ran a hand over her face, and Devlin took advantage of the moment to inspect her more fully. She had a wealth of ebony hair that fell in thick dreadlocks to her waist, the foremost of which were secured at the back of her head with a tie. Her almond-shaped eyes were obsidian jewels, set in a delicate face with clear skin just a hint too pale to be natural. A silver hoop pierced one nostril and the sharp horns that curled from her temples were also black, as were the tips of her fingers and her curved claws.

She was breathtaking, even in her simple, torn jeans and the snug navy tank that showed off flared hips, rippling muscles and breasts that, were he of a ravishing mind, Devlin had no doubt would fill his hands to bursting.

And, oh, the more he looked at her, the more he was of a ravishing mind.

"Regardless of who they're after, there are Hunters at my door," Jacinta said, her voice strained.

Reminded of the threat, Devlin turned towards the front of the shop as another explosion slammed into the windows. Though this one bore no shockwave thanks to the mage's shield spell, the entire building creaked and smoke obscured the street beyond.

Ivory sighed and dropped her hand. "You're right. We'll have to run."

"You don't want to fight?" Devlin frowned as he glanced between the two women. "You both seem skilled and I was once a Knight of the Round Table."

"A knight," Ivory repeated, disbelief thick in her voice.

"Yes."

"Without a head?"

"I ... Yes."

"Or armour."

"Indeed."

Ivory pursed her lips. "And your sword?"

"I didn't bring it."

"So, then, Sir Useless—"

"Devlin," he put in quickly, sketching a deeper bow than before. "Sir Devlin, my lady."

"*Sir* Devlin," Ivory drawled, leaning one hip against the counter. "I don't know how much experience you have with Hunters, but they're like a hydra; cut off one head and two more will spawn. When they return, they'll do so en masse, and Jacinta will lose everything." She drummed her fingers on the counter-top. "If we run, Jacinta can claim we attacked her and then fled."

"I'd never say that!" Jacinta thumped a fist against her chest. "This is my shop, and I offered you a safe space within it. If those Hunters think—"

"Stop. We both know this is pointless," Ivory snapped. "I won't have your death, or worse, on my conscience."

Jacinta pursed her lips, fine lines of strain developing at the corners of her eyes. "All right. I can buy you enough time to slip out the back, but that's about it."

Ivory nodded, and though her expression was firm, the look she shared with the mage was almost ... sad. "Thank you," she murmured. "For everything."

Jacinta nodded once, then lifted her arms. The two blue bands inked into her skin began to glow, the same light trickling from her fingertips as she traced arcane symbols in the air.

"Come on." Ivory grabbed Devlin's wrist and hauled him through the doorway behind the counter. "This way."

The back portion of the building consisted of two downstairs storage rooms, a short hall and a staircase, beneath which nestled an unassuming wooden door. Ivory released her grip on Devlin's arm to flatten herself against the wall, opening the door just enough to peer outside.

"It's clear for now, but that won't last." She flicked a glance over her shoulder. "Be ready to move, Sir Useless."

Devlin opened his mouth to reply but the words died in his throat as Ivory licked one of her fingers then drew it across the locking mechanism. Where her skin touched, she left a black smear that began to smoke and sizzle, melting the metal like so much candle wax.

"Amazing." Devlin edged closer, lifting his head to examine her handiwork. "How did you do that?"

Ivory didn't answer, striding through the door and into the open air beyond. Devlin followed her into a small courtyard nestled between the buildings. There was a herb box on one side and a two person outdoor setting on the other. Neatly swept pavers were bordered by a half-height brick wall which separated the back of the property from the narrow roadway beyond. He turned in time to see Ivory close the door, licking her finger to run a second black smudge over the outer edge of the metal security screen so that it, too, melted into the frame.

"My vehicle isn't far from here." Devlin pointed across the road where the RV's bulk could barely be seen through the trees. "If we can reach it, we can leave."

"That's not going to work." Ivory shook her head, long dreadlocks quivering as though they had a mind of their own. "The Hunters will have people watching any new or suspicious vehicles – assuming they weren't already tracking you before you arrived. You're better off cutting your losses while you can."

Devlin froze. "I can't leave my vehicle; Bailey's in there."

"So call Bailey and tell him to run for it," Ivory growled.

"Bailey is a she," Devlin huffed. "And I have no way to contact her apart from appearing in person. If we work together, you and I can overcome any trap the Hunters may have lain."

"What? Oh, no." Ivory leaped back as though burnt. "Considering you brought the Hunters down on my head and ruined what little of a life I've been able to create in this town, you're lucky I saved your ass back there as it is." She reached behind her, drawing the tie from her dreadlocks so that they tumbled around her face in gorgeous disarray. Devlin was so distracted by the silver clips and coloured beads woven into the foremost locks that he almost missed it when she said, "This is where we part ways, Sir Devlin."

There was no mistaking the bite of mockery in the way Ivory spoke his name. Devlin drew himself up to his full, headless height, adopting his haughtiest expression. "I will accept my fault in this matter, though I swear it was unintentional – but I must argue with your determination to part from me."

"Oh?" Ebony eyes drilled into his. "Because you need my help?"

"Yes," he admitted, "there is that. However, by your own admission, Hunters are not easily dissuaded. We stand a better chance of escape if we work together ... and I am worried for Bailey."

"Dammit." Ivory spat on the ground; her saliva shrivelled the grass where it landed. "I'm going to regret this; I just know it."

Devlin brightened. "You're going to help me?"

"And *you're* going to help *me*." She bared pointed teeth. "The deal is simple: I'll help you liberate Bailey and the RV if you agree to take me out of town, to a safe place of my choosing."

"Deal," Devlin offered his hand to seal the bargain, but Ivory merely raised a brow and stepped away. When she continued to watch him in silence, he sighed and dropped his arm. "Let's go."

Keeping his head tucked close to his chest and his body low, Devlin hurried across the road and into the trees that surrounded the RV. Ivory kept pace by his side, eyes partly narrowed and jaw clenched tight. Her movements were fluid and her steps silent, a feat that made Devlin feel like some sort of intruding brute stomping through the woods when, in reality, his own footfalls were so soft, most creatures would never hear them.

From the way Ivory kept glaring, she wasn't most creatures.

By the time they reached the small clearing where the RV was parked, he'd seen and scented three intruders; one high, watching from the limbs of an ancient tree, and the other two crouched deep in the underbrush on either side of the RV's single door, mostly camouflaged by their brown leathers.

When he glanced at Ivory – whose nose was raised to the air in a move that highlighted the length of her pale throat – she flared her nostrils and held up three fingers, pointing to each of the Hunters he'd already identified.

"No weapons," he mouthed. "You?"

Ivory flexed her fingers in such a way that he had no choice but to blink down at her claws – which grew as he watched, along with her horns, until they seemed far too large for her delicate head. The black of her irises bled outward, overtaking the whites and when she smiled, her pointed teeth were twice as long, barely contained within her mouth.

"Incredible," he breathed, rubbing at the sudden ache in his chest. Ivory was as deadly as she was beautiful, and he longed to pull her close and explore her altered features – but then she jerked her chin towards the Hunter in the treetops, reminding Devlin they'd come here for a reason.

He grunted an affirmative and began circling quietly through the trees towards the nearest of the Hunters on the ground. The man had a high-powered crossbow tucked under his chin, finger resting lightly on the trigger as he aimed at the RV's door.

Devlin smiled.

Time to demonstrate exactly what it meant to be a Knight of the Round Table.

DAMSEL IN DISTRESS

Leaving Devlin to handle the Hunters by the RV, Ivory shimmied up to the base of the tree, pausing to toe off her boots and let the claws on her feet grow to match the ones on her fingers. She should have walked away from the damnably handsome Sir Devlin when she had the chance – or, more accurately, tossed his ass out of Jacinta's shop the moment she'd heard him speaking demonic. Except she hadn't, and now she was here facing down Demon Hunters alongside a man whose head wasn't anywhere in the vicinity of his shoulders, all because she couldn't leave an innocent woman trapped inside the RV.

Bloody bleeding heart – will you never learn?

Swallowing her growl, Ivory dug her claws into the tree and began to climb. Her quarry perched about halfway up, his butt wedged in a sturdy fork while he straddled the thicker of two branches and stared through the scope on his crossbow. Ivory licked her left thumb as she drew level with his knees, causing the liniment on her claw to hiss and smoke. The Hunter gasped and twisted towards the noise, bringing the crossbow to bear with superhuman speed. Clenching the trunk between her thighs, Ivory blocked the weapon's progress and yanked on his wrist, bending the Hunter almost double so that she could wrap clawed fingers around his throat and sink her thumb into the flesh beneath his ear.

"Oops." She smiled as his eyes turned glassy. "That'll teach you, won't it?"

The Hunter's lashes slid shut, his body sagging in her grip. The crossbow tumbled from his hands and Ivory caught it before it could clatter against the trunk. Bracing against the tree, she wrestled the Hunter back into the same position she'd found him, then used his belt to tether the weapon further along the branch so that when he opened his eyes, he'd be staring at the poisoned tip on the end of the bolt. Licking one of her other claws, she wiped a cloudy smudge over the crossbow's firing mechanism. It automatically began to melt, crumpling until the weapon was completely unusable – though the Hunter wouldn't realise that when he woke up.

"Sweet dreams," she whispered and then, spotting Devlin in the clearing, dropped to the ground. By the time she straightened, her claws, teeth and horns had shrunk to their normal size.

"Did you kill him?" Devlin asked, waving a hand at the tree behind her.

"Of course." When he blinked, she snorted. "So gullible. No, he's not dead, just unconscious."

Devlin's dark brows beetled and Ivory was delighted to discover that he was just as handsome when annoyed. Perhaps more so, considering his eyes darkened and his jaw clenched, emphasising the scar on his cheek and the press of his lips against one another.

"You honourable warrior types are all the same," she muttered, rolling her eyes. "I'd like to point out that I'm not asking if you killed *your* allotted assholes or not."

His frown deepened. "Of course I didn't."

"Right. So, are you going to disapprove of me all day, or are we going to get out of here before these cockwads wake and we *do* have to kill them?"

Devlin shifted his head back and forth in his hands. Ivory would have bet everything she owned that he debated whether or not to climb the tree and see if the Hunter really was still breathing or not. In the end, he grunted and turned to the RV.

"Bailey?" he called. "I'm opening the door."

There was an oddly heavy thumping from inside the vehicle. Nodding in satisfaction, Devlin drew a key from his pocket, set it in the lock, and twisted. The door popped like a pressurised hatch, sliding aside to reveal the few steps into the RV. Ivory got a glimpse of the driver's seat and a set of overhead cupboards before an enormous black shape barrelled down the stairs and onto the grass.

"What in the world is *that?*" she demanded, unable to contain the utter astonishment in her voice.

Devlin raised an eyebrow. "That? You mean Bailey?"

"*That's* Bailey? I thought Bailey was your lover!" Ivory stared at the creature and shook her head.

The easiest word to describe Bailey was 'horse', though even as it popped up in her head, Ivory knew the term to be woefully inadequate. Bailey was taller and broader through the chest and shoulders than any horse Ivory had ever seen. Her coat, mane and tail were a shimmering, glossy black and her eyes the same pale, demonic lime green as Devlin's – only her pupils were slitted like a cat's, rather than round like a horse's should be. Her hooves were big enough to crush dinner plates and surrounded by long, silky fur that flipped and danced as she pranced in place, head high and nostrils dilated.

"My lover?" Devlin's whole body shook with laughter. "No, Bailey is my companion. Once, she was a destrier, the noblest of knightly steeds. But since the curse ..."

"Deathcharger," Ivory breathed, clasping her hands to her chest as Bailey opened her mouth to reveal long, pointed fangs. "Oh, she's beautiful. Aren't you, girl?"

Bailey postured and snorted smoke for another moment or

two, then, ears flattened against her head, extended her nose to sniff Ivory from hip to shoulder.

"She's very intelligent," Devlin began, looking somewhat ill as Bailey's fang-filled mouth came ever closer to Ivory's throat. "And can be somewhat ... ah ... temperamental."

"Hello, gorgeous," Ivory murmured, staring into Bailey's luminous gaze. "I know all about being called temperamental – it means people don't have the fortitude to handle us as we truly are. Don't listen to Sir Useless, hmm? You're perfect." She lowered her voice to a whisper. "We are kin, you and I."

Bailey made a sound that might have been a whinny, but for the echoing edge of a demonic squeal. She rubbed her cheek against the side of Ivory's head. With a laugh, Ivory threw her arms around the deathcharger's enormous neck.

"If you're finished making acquaintances," Devlin grumbled, "we shouldn't linger long."

Bailey snapped her teeth at him.

"Still displeased with me, I see."

The deathcharger rumbled, the sound so close to the spoken demonic language that Ivory strained to make sense of it.

"I did *not* bring the Hunters down upon us," Devlin protested, crossing his arms over his chest. "It was simple misfortune that they were in the area."

Ivory choked on a laugh, and Bailey snorted in blatant disbelief.

Devlin growled and stalked off towards the RV. "Fabulous. Now there are *two* of them."

Ivory buried her face in Bailey's mane to hide her laughter, and the deathcharger immediately used her giant head to tuck their bodies even closer together. Her soft, velvety nose moved over Ivory's dreadlocks, chest expanding as she drew deep lungfuls of her scent. After a while she made a noise that sounded an awful lot like, "Okay?"

"Yes, I'm okay." Ivory stepped back to offer her first real smile in years. "Though your master was nearly caught."

"No," Bailey huffed. "Friend."

Ivory's smile widened. "My mistake. Nobody lords over a deathcharger."

Bailey dipped her head in a nod but her eyes drifted towards the trees, one ear flickering. "Go."

"Are there more?" Ivory lifted her nose to the air but couldn't smell anything more than the sulphuric scent of demonic horse.

"Yes." Bailey nudged Ivory towards the RV. "Go."

Torn between the misery of fleeing – again – and the idiocy of making a stand, Ivory allowed herself to be herded into the RV, Bailey managing the steps by the simple expedient of jumping over them, her ridiculous bulk landing neatly inside with the temerity of a mountain goat.

Devlin was already in the driver's seat, head propped in his lap so that he could see where to insert the crystal key. Taking a seat on a nearby couch, Ivory watched in amusement as Bailey moved to the back of the vehicle, climbed onto the bed as though it were a dog mat and curled up with her legs tucked beneath her. The RV rumbled to life and Devlin hemmed and hawed over the instruments until he located the gearshift, put the thing in drive and lurched awkwardly forward.

"Stop!" Ivory shouted. The RV jerked up short, a small jet near Devlin's shoulder spitting a steady stream of water all over his chest.

"Again?" He patted ineffectually at his leather jacket. "Why is that pedal even down there?"

Ivory surged out of her chair. "Do you have any idea what you're doing? We almost ran into those trees!"

"I am relatively inexperienced with this vehicle," Devlin snapped. "I read the operating instructions but they made no sense and when I asked for advice, the woman ran away screaming."

Ivory covered her face with both hands and counted to ten. When she lowered them, she spoke as calmly as she knew how. "Get out of the damned chair. I'll drive."

She expected him to argue but instead, Devlin's face lit up. "You will? Wonderful! See, Bailey? Someone who can help us, at last!"

"I'm helping you get away from the Hunters so that I can also get away from the Hunters," Ivory reminded him, but it was impossible to stop the smile that flirted with her lips as Devlin scooped up his head and rocketed out of the driver's seat. "Once we're safe, we're going our separate ways."

Rather than moving to the comfortable couch as she'd anticipated, Devlin strapped himself into the passenger seat and angled his head so that he could watch Ivory put the RV in reverse and carefully back away from the pine trees looming in front of them. When she executed a three-point turn he applauded, eyes wide with boyish excitement.

The road was uneven but the RV's suspension was excellent, and Ivory accelerated with little more than a glance in the mirror to ensure everything was as it should be. They'd been driving a little over five minutes before she clicked her tongue against her teeth. "Damn. We're being followed."

Devlin unclipped his seatbelt and turned to kneel on his chair, lifting his head into the air so he could see out the back window. "A car and ... what are those smaller things?"

"Magebike," Ivory grumbled. Whoever decided to take the remnants of humanity's motorcycles and cram their engines full of power stones deserved to be hauled off and shot. Fast, silent and horrifically dangerous, magebikes were as likely to spark out their power cores and explode as they were to take their rider from point A to B, but for those more magically inclined beings – or ones with more ego than sense – they were a popular choice.

Ivory pushed the accelerator to the floor and the RV picked up speed as best it could. The sleek black car, flanked by the two magebikes as though they were starring in a movie, drew steadily closer and she gnashed her teeth. "They're going to catch us."

Devlin sighed. "So be it. Although this time, we may have little choice but to kill them."

"Well, duh. They're trying to kill us, after all."

"I'm glad we agree." He slid her a sideways glance. "Can you manage the vehicle in this situation? Because if so, Bailey and I will confront the Hunters."

"Manage the – what are you talking about?"

Devlin didn't answer, disappearing towards the back. When he returned a few moments later, he had a sword strapped to his shoulders and Bailey hard on on his heels. "Slow down a little, so they think they've caught us."

Mad. The man was utterly, utterly mad – but as he wedged his head on the dashboard, his nose pressed to the windscreen, Ivory lessened the pressure she was applying to the accelerator and the RV slowed.

Devlin stretched out a hand and Bailey immediately put her nose in it, giving him a reference point. She whuffed against his fingers and on the dash, Devlin's lips twisted into a smile. "Forgiven?"

Bailey nipped.

"Ah. Fair enough, I suppose."

Ivory wanted to ask what that meant but before she had a chance, the two magebikes shot past the RV and pulled in front of it, boxing the vehicle between themselves and the larger car behind. The RV's door slid open on a hiss and Ivory watched in astonishment as Bailey hopped down the steps and out onto the road as though the motor home were standing still.

"Bailey!" Ivory cried – but then the deathcharger was beside the open door, her long, silken mane flying in a wind of her own making, legs powering as she galloped. Bailey screamed, a sound of fearsome challenge that could never be mistaken for a neigh, and Devlin launched his body out the door without the slightest hesitation.

"You forgot your head!" Ivory gasped.

"Too annoying. I want both my hands," Devlin's head replied. "This will work just as well."

Bailey, who'd barely broken stride as she dipped her body to catch his, picked up speed as Devlin wrapped the fingers of one hand in her mane and bent low over her neck. He drew his sword as Bailey passed the front of the RV, and Ivory took a moment to admire the black hilt and curving crimson blade splashed with demonic runes.

She flicked a look at the speedometer and blinked. "Just how fast can Bailey go?"

"Faster than this."

True to his declaration, the deathcharger began to close on the nearest magebike. The Hunter on board glanced over his shoulder and startled as he spotted her – and the headless body on her back – but it was already too late. As Ivory watched, Bailey bit at the back tyre while Devlin swung his sword in a wide, flat arc, taking the Hunter's head from his body.

Devoid of a rider, the bike began to wobble. With a giant heave, Bailey tossed both bike and corpse aside, leaving behind a splatter of gore and a lone head, which bounced off the RV's front bumper and then rolled underneath.

Ivory laughed. "One down, two to go!"

Devlin grimaced. "Having been decapitated myself, I feel somewhat guilty."

"I don't see why – he's dead. He didn't feel me running his head over."

"You ... are a very unusual person." Devlin's eyes narrowed as Bailey swung closer to the other magebike. As she did, the Hunter raised his arm, a laser pistol extruding from his sleeve via the convenience of a mechanical holster. Devlin's scimitar flashed but the bike swerved aside and the laser levelled straight at Bailey's chest.

"Tell her to go faster," Ivory urged, planting her foot back on the RV's accelerator. The road curved ahead, and she cut through the inside of the corner to gain ground as Devlin's heels dug into Bailey's ribs.

Ivory could hear the Hunter laughing as he tracked the demonic horse with his laser. Echoing his laughter, she slammed the RV into the back wheel of his bike. It flipped up into the air, narrowly missing the top of the RV as it did so. The Hunter's laser discharged, the blue beam going wide as his arms and legs windmilled uselessly before he slammed into the trunk of a tree and slid to the ground.

With a grunt of effort, Ivory transferred her weight from accelerator to brake, bracing herself as the RV's wheels locked and it skidded across the asphalt in a giant cloud of smoke.

"Stay here," Ivory said, pulling on the handbrake.

"Not like I have much choice at the moment," Devlin muttered. "My body's still outside."

Ivory popped open the door and pulled herself onto the roof. Using the smoke as cover, she scuttled down the length of the vehicle, pausing at the end to peer over the lip. The Hunters' car had swerved to avoid a head-on collision and now rested flush against the back of the RV. As the passenger door cracked open, Ivory dropped onto the sedan's roof and lashed out with her claws. The Hunter who leapt from the vehicle shouted in surprise, two long, thin slices appearing along the side of his face as he sailed by. Pain contorted his features and he slapped both hands to his cheek, collapsing to the ground to scream and thrash as Ivory's poison ate steadily away at flesh and bone. Satisfied that he was no longer a problem, Ivory stuck her head and shoulders into the cabin of the car – where the driver had a crossbow levelled at the open door.

"I wouldn't," Ivory growled, her tongue thick in her mouth as her teeth and horns began to lengthen.

The woman's lips trembled but her grip on the crossbow firmed. "I have to."

"Why?" Digging her toe-claws into the roof, Ivory manoeuvred further inside. Upside down as she was, her dreadlocks draped over the car's gearshift and when she offered the Hunter a smile full of overly long, pointed teeth, the woman flinched. "I have no problem with you. Put the crossbow down, swear off, and I'll let you walk away."

"It's a Hunter's duty to cleanse the world of demonic filth," the woman whispered, her fingers tightening on the stock of her weapon. "To keep people safe."

"The people *you* decide are worth protecting, you mean?" Ivory flexed one hand, showing off her claws, and watched the Hunter swallow. "If you'd met me twenty years ago, you'd think I was human. *I* thought I was human. I lived a normal life, in a normal house, with parents and friends and all that other crap. Then one day the worlds merged and magic remade us into ... whatever we are now." She smiled again, this time more a baring of demonic fangs. "The funny thing is, I didn't feel any different on the inside until people like you became a problem."

"I'm not the problem." The woman's voice firmed. "I'm the solution."

Ivory slapped the nose of the crossbow as it fired, the bolt whizzing past one ear. Wrapping her free hand around the Hunter's throat, she shoved her back in her seat, claws digging deep enough to draw blood.

"I'm not a disease to be cured," Ivory hissed, as the colour began to drain from the Hunter's face. "I may not be perfect – but unlike you, I offered the chance to walk away."

Withdrawing her hand, Ivory plucked the crossbow from the Hunter's nerveless fingers and dismantled it with quick, practised movements. Dropping the pieces onto the floor of the car, she searched the woman's pockets as her eyes slid shut for the final time. With only lint and lip gloss to show for her efforts and the car so clean it might as well have been new, Ivory pulled herself back onto the roof to discover Devlin standing by the open door, head in one hand and sword in the other.

"Are you all right?" His pale eyes flicked down her body and back up again, and a kernel of warmth kindled in Ivory's chest when he didn't flinch at the sight of her altered features.

"I'm fine." Raising up to her knees, she craned her head to look over his shoulder at the Hunter on the ground. "Dead?"

"Dead," Devlin confirmed. "As is the one who collided with the tree."

"Are you sure?"

He hefted his scimitar. "Very."

"Hmm." Ivory bit her lip and brandished the purloined lip gloss. "We need to check for—"

"I did," he cut her off, brows drawn tight. "Nothing on any of them to say who was the intended target."

Sighing, Ivory shoved her demonic energy as far down as it would go, returning to her almost-human form. Hunters were well known for relying on the wrist devices they all wore, but since they were coded to the owner's energy signature, it would be impossible to get anything out of them.

"They'll keep coming," Devlin said softly. "And no matter who they were originally chasing, they're now aware of all three of us."

"I know." Ivory tugged on one of her dreadlocks and, not for any other reason than to fill the silence, added, "I've been avoiding them on and off for years."

Bailey stuck her head around the back of the RV and whickered softly.

"She's right. We should go." Jamming his sword into the scabbard across his back, Devlin offered his hand. "I know you wish to part company, but truly, we'd be safer if we stuck together. The Hunters will overpower us far too easily if we separate."

Ivory stared at his outstretched fingers as though she'd never seen them before. When was the last time someone had offered her such a common courtesy?

"Why?" she asked, tracing Devlin's sword calluses with the tip of one long claw.

He didn't even pretend to misunderstand. "Because I like you."

"Because you need my help," Ivory corrected, glaring down at him from her perch. "To break your curse."

30

Devlin's hand didn't waver as he caught her gaze with his. "I do need your help, Ivory. That is correct. But I'm offering my hand because we are the same; two warriors on the run from an evil disguised as a cure." His lips curved in a wicked grin. "And because I want the excuse to feel your skin slide against mine."

Ivory's jaw dropped. Was he ... *flirting* with her?

Warmth bubbled again in her chest and she swallowed, as though that would somehow push the odd sensation back into the abyss where the rest of her feelings languished. It stayed stubbornly put and after a long moment, she shook her head and placed her hand in his.

Devlin's skin was warm and dry, his fingers large and gentle as they curled around her paler ones and when she leaned her weight against him, hopping from the car to the ground, he didn't budge so much as an inch.

They stared at each other a long moment, then Devlin carefully withdrew his hand and made a flourishing gesture in the direction of the RV. "Your chariot, my lady."

More warmth, and gods help her, a smile. Ivory strode towards the RV in the hopes he didn't see it, but the rumbling chuckle behind her said she was far too late. Bailey waited by the RV's open door, ears pricked in their direction and head tilted to the side.

"Okay?" she whuffed.

"Yes." Ivory climbed into the RV, dropping into the driver's seat with a sigh. "I'm going to regret this. I just know it."

PENANCE FOR THE OVERZEALOUS

As the day wore on and the RV steadily covered ground, Devlin succeeded in eliciting two more smiles from Ivory and, on one occasion, a sound he suspected might have been a hastily stifled laugh. Each time, he felt like a man who'd been handed the keys to the kingdom and each time, when the burst of warmth in his chest began to cool, he sternly reminded himself that nothing good could come of his increasing attraction to the demon who was his only hope for salvation.

Perhaps that was part of his punishment, to endure so many years wishing for nothing more than a chance to repent and then, standing upon the cusp of such an event, to glimpse a creature rarer and more beautiful than anything he'd come across before.

Devlin studied Ivory's profile as she handled the RV with an expertise he could only dream of. She'd tugged the foremost of her dreadlocks back into a tie, emphasising the clarity of her profile, the curl of her horns and the thick sweep of long, dark lashes. The silver ring in her nostril caught the sunlight when she moved, sparkling as though a thousand tiny diamonds encrusted the surface and bringing light to the shadowed skin around her eyes. He longed to form her curves with his hands, to kiss the lips currently set in a pout whilst she stared at the almost incomprehensible instruments on the RV's dash. Once, her biting personality would have turned him off – along with her obviously demonic features – but now all he saw was fire and life and glorious woman, and though he was damned beyond all measure, Devlin couldn't help the frisson of need that had him adjusting his weight in the passenger seat for the fourth time in as many minutes.

When she glanced his way and raised a brow, he realised he'd been caught staring and cleared his throat. "My apologies. You're the first person other than Bailey I've had a conversation with in ... a long time."

"Hmm." Ivory turned back to the road, drumming her clawed fingertips on the wheel. "If I'm guessing correctly, you're the Headless Horseman from myth and legend: a creature cursed to haunt his forested hollow, who kills anyone foolish enough to enter. Yes?"

Devlin gaped. "There are *stories* about me?"

"You don't know?" This time, both brows went up. "Where have you been these last centuries?"

"Bound to a forested hollow," Devlin grumbled, crossing his arms over his chest. "And it's been millennia, not centuries. I should also like to add that I haven't killed anyone who hasn't tried killing me first." He tsked in the back of his throat. "You are the first being since my beheading who's bothered to enter into an actual conversation."

"Probably because nobody else was fluent in demonic," Ivory mused.

"How was I to know I was speaking demonic? Everyone sounds the same to me."

Her face scrunched into a frown. "Everyone?"

"Yes."

"So you understand this?"

"Of course."

"And this?"

"Indeed."

"How about this?"

"Light save me, woman, yes!" Devlin bared his teeth at her and, for some unknown reason, it made her grin in response. "You're simply repeating yourself."

"Actually, I spoke in three different languages and only one of them was demonic." She pursed her lips. "It appears whoever cursed you had the gift of tongues."

"You know the nature of my curse?"

"No." She turned her head to look him in the eye for a single, shattering second before turning back to the road. "Only the nature of demons – which is that in basic cursing, you transfer at least a little of yourself into the target. The stronger the curse, the more energy is required."

"And if the demon who cast the curse died shortly afterwards?"

Ivory shot him another look, this one through half-shuttered lashes. "How exactly did your curse come about?"

"I thought you weren't interested," Devlin replied, adjusting his head where it rested on his lap.

"In breaking it? Not in the least." She checked the mirror, then the road, then the mirror again. "It's dangerous work and I've no reason to risk my neck for you."

"Not even if it's the right thing to do?"

Ivory snorted. "Nobody does the right thing anymore, Devlin. Honour, decency, morality? They're just words. Shields people use to justify whatever action will get the result they desire, all while crushing those they deem lesser beneath their shiny, self-righteous boots."

Devlin's jaw dropped. "Who wronged you so badly that you'd have such a view of the world?"

"Everyone," she said firmly. "It's easy enough for you – as long as your head's on your shoulders, you still look human. Me? I look like the monster under the bed that everybody loves to hate." Ivory glanced in the mirror and grimaced. "Speaking of monsters, there are Hunters up our ass again. You might want to hold on to something."

Devlin snatched his head against his chest, twining his fingers in his unruly hair for good measure. Ivory spun the steering wheel hard to the left and the RV began to skid, tilting precariously until Devlin braced one foot against the wall in an effort to stay upright. Bailey shrieked in the back, her hooves thumping against the cupboards as she sought to keep her place on the bed, adding to the cacophony of clattering plates and clanging pots that echoed in the space.

A concussive blast hit the side of the RV and the vehicle shuddered before it launched sideways into the air. For a moment Devlin was weightless, held in place by the seating restraint until gravity reasserted itself and the RV hit the ground roof-first, sliding along the road with a great shriek of metal and a dancing array of bright sparks.

"Move," Ivory shouted, somehow crouched neatly on the roof as if it had always been the floor. "We need to get out of here before they hit us again."

Suiting word to action, she raced on all fours towards the rear of the vehicle, where furious whinnying and thumping heralded Bailey's attempts to free herself from beneath the overturned mattress. After a cursory glance to ensure neither female was seriously injured, Devlin turned his mind to the rather knotty problem of removing his restraint. With his full body weight against the straps, the fastening mechanism was reluctant to release and with his head clasped in only one hand, it was difficult to—

"I said *move*," Ivory growled, appearing at his side.

Claws flashed, the straps went alarmingly slack and Devlin thumped shoulder-first into the ceiling-come-floor, his head clutched protectively against his gut. Something large and cold smacked into his rump and when he finally managed to extricate himself from the trap of his own limbs, Devlin realised it was his sword.

"Are you always this slow?" Ivory's head and shoulders appeared from behind a set of cupboards. Her brow furrowed as she looked beyond him. "Ah, fuck."

Claws flashed again, only this time they wrapped around Devlin's ankle, the curved tips digging into his boots as Ivory yanked him across the floor, sword and all, and then tossed him through a broken window and onto the street. He hit the ground and rolled in a clatter of blade and body parts, and before he'd had quite the chance to work out what was going on, Bailey threw her not inconsiderable weight on top of his.

An enormous explosion rent the air, accompanied by the squeal of twisting metal and the unmistakable *whomph* of an oil fire. Fighting against the warmth of Bailey's undercarriage, Devlin angled his head in time to see an enormous blue fireball arc into the sky.

"Get up!" Ivory's voice faded in and out through the crackle of the flames and the thumping of half-melted debris as it peppered the area. "Run!"

Bailey rolled upright and Devlin succeeded in getting to his feet, slinging his sword harness over one shoulder and hastily buckling it at the waist. The burning wreckage of the RV spilled smoke and fumes into the afternoon sky, but it was the silhouettes of many, *many* figures on the other side of the crackling furnace that had Devlin wrapping his hand in Bailey's mane to vault astride her back. Ivory leapt up behind him, arms wrapping tight around his waist, her body fitting to his like a second skin.

"We need to find somewhere safe," Devlin announced, closing his eyes against the sickening blur of trees and sky as Bailey launched into motion.

Behind him, Ivory's body rippled in a long, gusty sigh. "I know a place – and if we can get there, I can throw the Hunters off our trail."

Though her reluctance was palpable, Devlin's heart stirred hopefully at the offer. Prodding at the opening as one might pick the scab from a forming wound, he said, "I thought you wanted to part ways?"

"I do – but the Hunters are categorised by their magical ability to track a target no matter the distance. If we split up, I can clear my own trail, but they'd still track you – and when they catch you, they'll be able to use their skills to regain *my* trail. I don't have the time or energy to cleanse my magical signature morning and night on the offchance that I'm being pursued, so it makes more sense to cleanse everyone before we part company." Her arms tightened around his waist in warning. "And we *will* be parting company."

"Of course," Devlin said, as mildly as he knew how. "You've made it clear you wish nothing to do with me and my curse. I will not inconvenience you any more than I already have."

Ivory growled deep in her chest, an intriguing sound that caused her entire body to vibrate where it was pressed against Devlin's. He fought not to lean back into her, something dark and feral deep inside urging him to answer the sound in kind – as though they weren't people but beasts, creatures of some unknown shadowy plane who had a connection that went beyond society's decorous norms.

As though they were demons.

Bailey's haunches bunched and she leapt over some small obstacle, jostling Devlin so that he had to steady his head where it rested between his thighs. The action had a dry laugh bubbling in his throat – here he was mooning over a beautiful woman, when his head wasn't even attached to his shoulders. Even were he not a walking debt to be repaid, how could he ever hope to attract the interest of another when his head fell off every time he sneezed?

Fool.

Bailey snorted and began to shorten stride, muscles tensing as though for battle. Devlin opened his eyes to see a man on a white horse standing in their way. The sunlight shone off his white leathers so brightly Devlin had to squint. He caught the impression of blonde hair and broad shoulders before Bailey propped and reared, hundreds of years of training and instinct pulling her up short of the arrow that thunked into the ground in front of her.

Devlin glanced down at the arrow, stomach knotting. That was no crossbow projectile but a proper arrow, the fletchings coloured in a pattern he'd not seen since he was human.

"What's going on?" Ivory began to loosen her grip, but Devlin clamped his free arm over the top of hers to prevent the movement.

"Stay seated," he warned. "I cannot die, but you do not have the same luxury."

Bailey dropped back to all fours, neck arched and lip curled to reveal long, deadly teeth. The man on the opposite side of the clearing urged his horse forward with his knees, all the while raising his longbow and notching another arrow to the string. As he moved from light to shadow, his face came into view; strong jaw, golden beard, blue eyes that had once danced with merriment but were now hard and cold.

"Greetings, Gawain." Devlin angled his sword as Bailey pranced, putting herself – and the blade – between the man and Ivory. "I had not thought we would ever meet again."

For a moment Devlin feared his old friend wouldn't understand demonic, but then Gawain blinked and shook his head. "*Devlin?* I thought you dead."

"I should be." Devlin shrugged, the movement drawing attention to his headless shoulders. "Perhaps I am, for I'm certainly not alive."

Ivory's chin dug into one of those headless shoulders as she levered upward. "Who's this guy?"

"Ivory, may I present to you Sir Gawain, High Knight of the Round Table under King Arktur – you would, perhaps, know him as King Arthur – of the fae."

"Fae?" Ivory dug her talons into Devlin's ribs as she shifted for a better view. "I thought Arthur was King of England or something like that."

"The stories of my uncle which circulate this pustule of a realm are little more than hearsay and blasphemy," Gawain snapped. "The Round Table is long sundered and though Arktur still reigns over Camelot, I have not seen it in many a year. These days I am known as Gawain Braybrook, Master of Hunters and Head of the Healing Hall."

"Braybrook." Ivory's voice coiled along the ground, rustled through the leaves of the trees, every syllable dripping dark menace. "I know your people. I know what they do. I've lost family to the Hunters who prowl the night like cowards, stealing children from their parents and knifing innocents in their sleep – all for the supposed crime of their birth."

Gawain's blue eyes narrowed and he nudged his horse a step to the left, trying to get a better view of the woman tucked behind Devlin. "You're a Whitehaven."

The sound Ivory made was not a sound Devlin had ever heard made by anyone in his entire existence. Somewhere between a hiss and a growl, with the odd echo of a snapping fire and the cadence of a gale as it whistled through a lonely canyon – it was all of those things and none of them, and it made the hairs on the back of his neck rise and the infernal thing rooted in his gut blossom like a flower before the morning sun.

"I am no-one and nothing but myself," she breathed, the voice Ivory's and yet not; deeper, more guttural, accented in a way that even Devlin noticed. "You have no right to judge me."

Gawain snorted and drew his bow. "Judgement is unnecessary. You are a monster and I am oath-bound to cleanse this land of your filthy taint."

He let go the string.

Devlin twisted, yanking Ivory behind him a moment before the arrow thudded deep into his chest, shoving them both backwards. He wheezed as the projectile dug deep, the impact not painful so much as inconvenient. Ivory's body braced his and he used her strength to rock back upright, tossing his head at Gawain with a well-practiced flick of his arm.

Acting on instinct, the Hunter dropped his bow to catch the head, and Devlin immediately sank his teeth into the calloused thumb pressed against his lips. Gawain swore and shook his arm as though it were on fire, setting Devlin's eyes rolling inside his skull. Blood coated his tongue, his teeth slipped and quite suddenly his head was flying through the air, a dizzying spectacle of light and shade that was likely to end with a broken nose – until clawed fingers twisted into his hair and his cheek was tucked firmly against a pair of spectacular breasts.

"Can you see?" Ivory demanded. She'd risen to her feet on Bailey's back, braced with one hand planted firmly over the grisly stump of Devlin's neck. Though she cradled his head against her chest, it was only a few inches higher than if it was still attached to his body, giving Devlin not only a clear view of the situation but excellent depth perception to boot.

"Yes," he answered, and swung his sword.

Gawain's horse, nowhere near as skilled as Bailey, was too slow to dodge. Devlin's blade bit high into the stallion's shoulder and he jerked backwards with a scream, spraying blood all over Bailey's face and neck. Gawain swore and snatched at the reins but the moment Devlin pulled his sword free, the horse turned and bolted into the forest.

"Prey?" Bailey asked, eyes narrowed as she licked blood from her lips.

"Not today. We might beat Gawain if we work together, but the other Hunters will find us soon enough." Devlin sheathed his sword down his back, took a firm grip on the arrow buried in his chest and snapped the shaft off close to his body. "Safety is still the better choice – for now."

Shifting her grip on his stump of a neck, Ivory swung a leg over his shoulder and Devlin found himself with a sudden lapful of woman, his head sandwiched between their chests and no amount of clothing in the world capable of mitigating the sudden intimacy of their position.

"East," Ivory said, her tone distracted as she bent to inspect the place where the arrowhead was embedded in Devlin's pectoral. "Go east, Bailey."

With little more than a snort and a tail flick, Bailey moved again, her long, powerful legs and sure stride making for a smooth ride despite the lack of saddle or tack.

"Does it hurt?" Ivory asked, peeling his jacket open.

"Yes," Devlin admitted. With her breasts supporting his cheek, her sleek form draped over the top of his larger one and nowhere remotely appropriate to put his hands, how could he not be in pain? He cleared his throat as best he could and tried to keep a grip on Bailey's mane without accidentally grabbing, touching, brushing or poking anything he hadn't been invited to. "I've been shot through the heart."

"I see that." Ivory shifted Devlin's head to their combined laps so that she could have the use of both hands. "I need to dig this out. You're not going to pass out on me, are you?"

"Will you toss me to the side of the road if I do?"

Ivory chuckled, the first real laugh he'd heard from her throat. "You know I will."

"I hate to disappoint you, then, for I wasn't known to swoon even when I was alive."

She chuckled again, face softening as she probed gently at the raw edges of the wound. Cradled in the valley of their thighs, Devlin was somewhat mortified to discover he sported an increasingly enthusiastic erection that, thanks to the location of his own head, was poking him in the chin. What would Ivory do if she noticed? Castrate him, most likely – and though the notion made Devlin wince, his body steadfastly refused to cease craving her touch. And when she glanced at him from beneath long lashes, dark eyes overly large in the shadowed contours of her finely boned face ... well, it was enough to make a man who'd renounced his faith begin to pray all over again.

HOME IS WHERE THE SPIRITS HAUNT YOU

TWICE IVORY DECIDED NOT to take Devlin to the one place in the world that was sacred to her, but each time she changed her mind, inevitability changed it back again.

It wasn't that she felt obliged to keep her word; honour was no longer a moralistic illusion she bothered with. It wasn't even that Devlin needed her help – that much had been obvious from the minute his head fell off in the middle of Mystic Madhouse. It wasn't even because, though she'd die before she admitted it, she could feel the frayed edges of his demonic energy licking against hers, begging to be fixed.

It was, to her ever-increasing chagrin, because she liked him.

As Bailey approached the final rise before the protective wards, Ivory clenched her teeth against the urge to simply dismount and walk away. Enjoying someone else's company was dangerous. Liking them? Potentially fatal – and Ivory was done, *done*, with having her life threatened by her pathetic heart.

And yet here they were, proving her a liar of the highest calibre.

Bailey drew up short, snorting, and Ivory reached forward to smooth her fingers through the deathcharger's silky black mane.

"What is ..." Behind her, Devlin's voice trailed off and she could almost taste his confusion. They'd ridden most of the way facing one another so that Ivory could dig the Hunter's arrow out of his heart, but once it was done, she'd turned around, nestling her smaller body into the cradle of Devlin's thighs. He was nowhere near as warm as a human man but his bulk was comforting – not that she needed such a thing – and he smelled of cinnamon and sandalwood, two of her favourite spices to throw in the fire when the nights grew icy.

"Wait here," Ivory said, ignoring his question in favour of sliding to the ground. Patting Bailey's jaw on the way past, she moved through the first layer of wards and into the second, where she crouched to dig her claws into the dirt and let her eyes slide shut.

The land whispered, thousands of barely-heard voices melding together into a disjointed whole. Tracing the lines that bordered her small slice of safety, Ivory ensured no-one had tried to gain access before pulling her fingers free and moving back towards Bailey and Devlin. "I need a drop of blood from each of you so that I can attune the wards to let you pass."

"All right." Devlin drew a dagger from his jeans and used it to prick his thumb, dripping dark blood onto Ivory's outstretched palm. The moment the liquid touched her skin, lightning shot through Ivory's veins and she drew a sharp breath. There was so much chaos in Devlin's energy that it took everything to avoid being overcome – how was he still standing, let alone walking around? She blinked in a vain effort to clear her vision, ignoring the slap of demonic power in favour of letting it wash over her like water crashing into a pool far below. By the time she had a handle on the influx of energy, Devlin had used the same dagger to prick Bailey's shoulder and Ivory hurried to catch the welling blood before it dribbled to the earth.

The deathcharger's essence was much calmer, her blood a demonic black with an oily sheen – a mirror image for Ivory's own. She frowned as it mixed with Devlin's, the two energies telling her far more about their curse than Ivory wanted to know. Still, there was no other way to let them through the wards, so she pushed her instinctive understanding away and walked back through the layers of magic, pausing between the first and second barriers to carefully anoint each of her dirt-encrusted claws with a mixture of their essences. That done, Ivory once more buried her fingers in the dirt. The air around her shimmered as the barriers shifted and stretched, settling back into place with a contented hum.

Bailey snorted, ears twitching.

"You feel the change?" Ivory asked. When the deathcharger nodded, she allowed a small smile. "They like to be fed."

Devlin's face twisted but Bailey merely chuckled deep in her chest and stepped forward, the wards sliding over her and Devlin with a welcoming touch. Ivory shook the dirt from her hands and stood, leading them down the rise and past the third and final barrier which protected her home.

She heard Devlin gasp but didn't look back, enjoying instead the sight of her little slice of paradise. A cottage rose from the ground as though it had struggled free from great bonds, the walls and roof bunched and gnarled in a cattywampus collection of wood and stone. Overgrown gardens mingled with the natural growth of the forest, spreading out like the train of an elegant gown, and crawling up the walls and over the cottage roof with the tenacity of a spider's thick silk. The trees inside the wards bore leaves the perpetual colour of autumn, offsetting the dark green moss that blanketed the ground and lower walls of the cottage. A small, sturdy well crouched to one side of the front door, the bucket overturned on the stone lip and the sharply pointed roof as crooked as the cottage's.

"This is my home," Ivory said, filling her tone with warning. "My grandmother left it to me when she died."

"It's lovely," Devlin choked out.

"Your sincerity is overwhelming," Ivory muttered, swinging back to face him. "I realise it's not a castle, but – are you *crying?*"

The headless knight sat astride his demonic horse with his head cradled loosely in both hands, twin streaks of silver making his cheeks shine.

"I'm not sure I can find the words, but—" He sniffled, pale green eyes glassy as they met with hers. "It's been a long time since a place has welcomed me with such open affection. I'm honoured you have brought me to your home, Ivory. This is a truly sacred place and I will be forever grateful to have seen it."

They stared at each other, Ivory's tongue frozen as she tried to decide between softness and scorn. It was dumb, dumb, *dumb* to let down her walls but how could she not, when Devlin's words echoed how she'd felt herself the first time – and every time since – she'd arrived at the cottage? The thrumming energy of the land inside the wards called to her like nothing else and she'd been braced to hate Devlin invading her sanctuary … but he fit. Tall and broad and oh-so-alone on Bailey's midnight back, he was dark and real in a way nothing in her life had been for a long time. His tears were ridiculous and by all rights, she should laugh at him – but she stayed silent as her feet took her forward, as her hands lifted to cup Devlin's jaw. When she tugged, he let go, and she burrowed her clawed fingers into his hair as she raised his face to hers.

Ivory had never been much of a romantic but she did believe in following her instincts and right now, they demanded Devlin. As though in a dream, she let her lashes drift shut as she tilted her head down, brushing her lips over his in a gentle, questioning caress. When he didn't protest, she did it again, delighted when his mouth opened in blatant invitation.

With his head unattached to his body, it was up to Ivory to control their kiss, but as soon as she touched her tongue to Devlin's he more than made up for the passive nature of his state. Her fingers tightened in his hair as they devoured each other, tongues dancing and lips locked in a routine as old as the stars. Heat crawled over Ivory's skin and she pressed her body against Devlin's leg, his large hand gripping tight to her shoulder. It was an odd disconnect, his body on Bailey's back and his head in Ivory's hands, but it was equally as intoxicating to think he trusted her – *her* – enough to surrender his passion into her care. Nobody had ever done that before, and the enormity of it broke something inside her, something squishy and warm and dangerous. Ivory ended the kiss on a growl, her eyes flying open to meet Devlin's equally wide ones. His pupils had expanded until there was only a sliver of bright, infernal green remaining, his sharp cheekbones brushed with a delicate layer of pink.

"Sorry." Ivory cleared her throat. "I ... I shouldn't have done that."

She pushed Devlin's head back into his hands and he fumbled, catching at her wrist instead. "Wait. It's okay; I wanted you. It. That. For us."

"You did?"

"I'd be a liar if I didn't say I've wanted to kiss you since we first met." His smile was tentative, but the fire in his eyes was ferocious. "I just didn't think you'd welcome it, since my head and my body are ... somewhat disconnected."

"Somewhat?" Ivory snorted a laugh, and though the stubborn part of her screamed to wrench free of his grip, she drifted closer to Bailey's side. With the deathcharger's height and Devlin's head on his knee, they were almost eye to eye. "I still should have asked first. I am, after all, a demon."

He cocked an eyebrow. "You think that makes a difference?"

"Of course it does." Ivory dropped her gaze, slamming the door on the unpleasant memories which tried to surface. "We need to go inside so I can clear our magical trail. The wards will throw the Hunters off, but not for long."

She pulled on her arm and Devlin let go, dismounting from Bailey in one swift, smooth motion. As Ivory turned towards the house, he caught her shoulder and stepped around in front, raising his head by the hair until they were face height.

"I'm grateful for your help," he murmured, expression serious, "especially when I know you didn't want to give it. And, for what it's worth, I think you're beautiful."

Ivory grunted and ducked under his arm, hurrying towards the house to hide the way her cheeks heated. She'd kissed him on a whim and it had been wonderful – but looking him in the eye afterwards and hearing him say sweet things? Yeah, not her style. Besides, if what she'd gleaned from the confrontation with Gawain was correct, Devlin had once been a demon hunter in his own right; there was no way any attraction he felt was more than dread curiosity. Bitter resentment curdled her stomach and Ivory flattened a palm over her abdomen as she shouldered the front door open.

The interior of the cottage was warm and homey, with thick, plush carpets, wood-panelled walls and brightly lit rooms that smelled of the autumn forest. Her furniture, too, was hand-made from things the forest provided, the gnarled wood sanded until it was smooth and carved with illustrations and symbols before being polished to a welcoming sheen.

Leaving Devlin to explore on his own, Ivory made straight for the kitchen, her favourite place in all the world. To maximise space, the interior of the cottage was mostly open plan, with the enormous kitchen bench providing the central focus of the room. Made from a fallen tree whose trunk had been sliced to reveal the gorgeous rings inside, it appeared to have grown from the floor and was sealed and varnished with a combination of elbow grease and magic. The tree's trunk extended up one of the kitchen walls, a long branch stretching over the benchtop to provide the perfect place for Ivory to hang her favourite mugs and the smaller pots she used most often. Though the rest of the kitchen was more conventionally made, the cupboards and benches were of the same wood and blended seamlessly with the tree so that it appeared the entire room was inside a hollowed-out trunk.

After taking a moment to run her fingers across the benchtop in silent greeting, Ivory washed the dirt from her hands, unhooked her kettle and set it atop the wood stove. Dropping into a crouch, she tugged open the door to the firebox, licked the pinky finger on her left hand and drew a demonic rune on the large central log. The rune immediately began to glow, then smoulder, then, with a pop, caught alight. Powered by magic, the fire spread swiftly through the box and in a matter of seconds the entire woodpile was ablaze.

Ivory shut the door and straightened to find Devlin on the opposite side of the bench, head cradled in the crook of his elbow and a look of astonishment on his handsome face.

"What?" Ivory snapped, going on tiptoe to unhook two large mugs and a small cast iron pot. "I need tea, and we need to get started on the trail cleanser."

"You ... you just ..." Devlin drew in the air with his free hand. "And then it caught fire."

Ivory opened her pantry, stepping into the cramped space to avoid seeing his expression. "My magic is different from other demons."

"Why?"

"Because *I'm* different from other demons."

"Different how?"

"None of your business." Drawing a deep breath, she focussed on the spell to cleanse their magical trail and let the ingredients whisper to her in response. She'd done this ritual before, of course, but now that Devlin was involved, Ivory suspected some tweaks would need to be made. Ah, yes: the duskshroom was singing over the loamroot, and the carrowshire powder was bowing out in favour of the fickleweed.

The man at her bench was silent as Ivory made several trips to and from the pantry, stacking jars on the bench until she had everything she needed. By that time the kettle whistled, so she poured two mugs of tea and offered one to Devlin.

"I wish I could drink it," he said, looking mournfully into the mug.

"You can't eat or drink?"

He raised an eyebrow. "Whatever I swallow goes down my throat, which isn't connected to the rest of me. It's ... messy."

Ivory blinked. "I didn't think of that."

"Me," whinnied Bailey from the door. "Meeeee."

It seemed impossible that the deathcharger would fit through the doorway but Bailey appeared unconcerned by the laws of physics, her enormous bulk contracting and expanding in a decidedly uncomfortable-looking phenomenon until she stood inside the cottage. While Ivory's mind tried to adjust to what she'd just witnessed, the deathcharger picked her way around the lounge room furniture and then curled up on the rug in front of the fireplace like an enormous, infernal hound.

"Me," she repeated, bright eyes filled with hope as they locked on the spare mug in Ivory's hand. Her black ears flickered. "Pleeeeease?"

There was that word again. Please. Ivory wavered between irritated and charmed, but in the end charmed won. She tipped Devlin's tea into a bowl and rounded the bench, setting it by Bailey's front legs. "Here you go, beautiful."

Bailey whickered in delight, lifting her face to lip affectionately at Ivory's jaw. "Thanks."

"Welcome." Ivory laughed, smoothing the silky black forelock back from Bailey's forehead. "Someone might as well enjoy it with me."

When she returned to the kitchen, Devlin's expression had turned sour, his jaw a hard line. Choosing to ignore him, Ivory took a bracing sip of her own tea – a blend of leaves and spices she'd grown and dried herself – and went to the sink. Instead of rinsing her hands as she'd done before, she drew out a small bristled brush and her home-made, magically enhanced soap, and set to scrubbing. For several minutes she worked in silence, until at long last Devlin moved into the kitchen to stand beside her.

"What are you doing?"

"Washing my hands," Ivory answered, flexing her fingers to

49

better display the rapidly blackening suds. "The ritual won't work if I've got other magic in play."

"Other ..." Devlin trailed off as she turned the tap on and rinsed, black suds disappearing down the drain to reveal her clawed fingertips in their natural, too-pale-to-be-human shade. "I thought your skin was meant to be that way."

Ivory considered telling him to mind his own business a second time. He was, after all, not her problem. Though as the minutes ticked by, she started to worry that the situation wasn't as simple as she'd hoped. With a sigh, she relented and shook her head. "When I leave the safety of the wards, I go prepared. I can't do magic like other demons can, and for a long time I thought I didn't have any. It was only once I moved here and started going through the library that I came across reference to ... different kinds of demons. I discovered that I could make potions and liniments and the like, and they'd serve as a conduit for my magic when I wasn't in my full demon form."

"A conduit?"

"Yes." When he blinked, she smiled wide enough to show off all her pointed teeth. "Let's say I make a liniment for fire. I coat the tip of one finger, letting it soak into the skin as it dries. It's dormant in that state – until I use my saliva, sweat or blood to activate the magic. Sometimes I draw runes to focus the spell but usually I just lick the finger I need and get on with it."

"Like when you melted the magic shop's door."

"Yes."

"Huh." Devlin stared at her hands for a moment, then smiled. "Clever."

Unsure what to do with the compliment, Ivory shrugged and dried her now clean hands before returning to the bench. The potion for cleansing her magical trail was a familiar one and she barely stopped to think as she portioned ingredients into the small pot, added some water and a generous dash of brandy, then set it on the stove where the kettle had been.

"A demon who makes potions," Devlin muttered to himself.

Ivory glanced over her shoulder to find his brow furrowed, gaze distant. "I wonder if that's what she was."

"Who?"

He sighed. "The demon who cursed me. She was picking herbs and mushrooms in the forest when I ..."

"Slaughtered her?"

"Yes." Devlin's lashes drifted shut and he grimaced. "That is as good a term for it as any."

Something shifted in the air, a subtle humming in the atmosphere that had Ivory looking around her in surprise. "She was."

"What?"

"She was like me – her magic, I mean," Ivory amended.

Devlin's eyes flew open, his jaw slack with shock. "You ... how do you know that?"

Ivory set one hand against the cottage wall. "She told me."

"She's *here?*" He spun around, but there was nobody other than Bailey, who'd finished her tea and gone to sleep.

"Not in the sense you're thinking." Ivory picked up a wooden spoon and stirred the mixture on the stove. "This place is sacred to my family; it's been part of our heritage since Mu and Earth first began to merge. When we die, our spirits ... I suppose you might say they leave an echo here. It's not their actual ghost, more a spiritual residue that helps replenish the magic in the land and power the wards. Sometimes the echoes resonate with a certain statement or item, and if I listen hard enough I can glean information from them."

Devlin whistled between his teeth. "Is that the power of ... what did Gawain call you? The Whitehavens?"

Ivory froze, clenching the handle of the spoon so tightly that her claws pierced her palm. She wrenched her hand back lest her blood fall into the mixture and ruin it, moving quickly to the sink to wash until the bleeding stopped.

"I'm not a Whitehaven," she hissed, wiping her hands vigorously on a towel.

"All right," Devlin said, his tone easy. "I apologise. I know nothing of the word, or what it means, only that Gawain called you—"

"The Whitehavens are a family of demons, led by Lord Luthier Whitehaven. He protects demons who wish to live in peace and polices any demons who wish to harm others." Ivory tossed the towel in the sink. "They also rescue – or try to – anyone captured by the Braybrooks."

"Gawain, you mean?"

"Yes and no. The Braybrooks are a family almost as old as the Whitehavens. They purport themselves as healers but only heal those they deem worthy of their services – and the healing always costs more than mere coin. They're the driving force behind the Hunters, who are zealots of the worst kind."

"Gawain ... I knew he hated demons, but to foster such bigotry ..." He clicked his tongue against his teeth. "What happened to him that he would discard all honour and become such a villain?"

"No-one knows and to be frank, nobody cares. You might know Gawain as a knight in shining armour, but these days?" Ivory spat in the sink. "He's laughing as he dirties his hands."

Silence thickened the atmosphere and Ivory cursed herself for speaking so honestly. Stepping around Devlin, she returned to the stove, bending to sniff the mixture before removing it from the heat.

"You know an awful lot about this for someone who lives in a hermit's cottage in the forest," Devlin said at last. His tone was soothing rather than accusatory, the low timbre of his voice vibrating through Ivory's bones until she shut her eyes to soak it in.

"I was human, once, you know." A dry chuckle rattled in her throat. What was that saying in her grandmother's journals? In for a penny, in for a pound? "I was a young girl with hopes and dreams. That all changed when the worlds merged and I suddenly found myself overtaken by demonic blood I never knew I had. My parents did the best they could, but they believed in common decency and the world was in chaos." Ivory curled her lip. "They were killed within a week, and I was left alone at fourteen years old."

"Ivory ..." Devlin took a step towards her, but she held up a hand in warning.

"I learned to fend for myself but after two years, a team of Hunters found me. I thought I was going to die – even when a man and woman showed up to rescue me." She blinked, caught in the memory of that moment, then shrugged. "They were Whitehavens."

"They took you in," Devlin guessed.

"They did." Ivory nodded. "I returned with them to the Whitehaven's estate, and even met the great Lord Luthier. He told me I wasn't just a demon, but one with Whitehaven blood – from my grandmother's side, apparently. He insisted that demons like them could assume a human form as well as their demonic form, and that with training and practice, I'd be able to as well." She barked a harsh laugh. "I trained for five years, worked alongside the people I thought were my new family, but what you see now is as human as I could get. I told myself it didn't matter what I looked like and kept working, focussing every waking moment on becoming one of the fabled Whitehavens who fought for equality for all."

"What happened?" Devlin put out a hand, and this time, Ivory didn't protest when he caught her wrist and gently tugged her closer.

"Others who trained alongside me were sent into the world while I remained in the compound. I waited until Luthier next came to visit and confronted him, demanding to know when I'd get my chance." Her lips pinched, and resentment burned like acid in her blood. "Lord Whitehaven ever so gently explained that though my fighting skills were exceptional, my appearance frightened people. Without any discernible magic and lacking the ability to transform, he feared I'd do irreparable damage to the Whitehaven name if I were sent into the world."

Devlin rumbled deep in his chest, a thick, menacing sound that set Ivory's heart racing even as she refused to look at him, fearing the pity she'd see on his face.

"I hope you fought," he growled. "I hope you proved how wrong he was."

"Yes ... but not in the way you're assuming."

"Oh?"

"I decided that if people thought me a monster, then I would become one." Ivory glanced at him at last, an evil smile tugging the corners of her lips as she dared Devlin to judge her. "I set fire to the training rooms in the middle of the night and while those goody-two-shoes were running around trying to put it out, I snuck into Luthier's office, stole everything of value that wasn't nailed down, and left."

"And came here?"

"Not straight away." Ivory inspected her now clean claws, her voice soft. "I ran from both the Whitehavens and the Braybrooks for almost a year, pawning items from the loot I'd taken whenever I could find someone whose greed overcame their revulsion at my appearance. Eventually, down near the bottom of the sack, I found a stone talisman wrapped in a pigskin map. The characters were strange but the more I stared at them, the more they became legible – until I realised I held the keystone to the wards for this cottage. It was a long journey, but the moment I crossed the wards and felt the spirits singing to me, I knew I was home."

Devlin frowned. "Nobody followed you?"

"I don't know," Ivory admitted, shrugging. "The cottage was a shambles when I arrived, having had nobody to occupy it for so long. I spent the first night in the library as it was the only protected room, and the spirits guided me to my grandmother's journal, where I found the spell for cleansing my magic trail. This spell," she added, picking up the pot and carefully cupping the outside to see if the mixture had cooled. "It was the first one I ever cast, cobbled together from the few ingredients that remained in the pantry. When it worked, I realised that for all his knowledge, for all his long life, Lord Luthier Whitehaven had been wrong; I had magic, it was just different." Ivory tilted her head to the side. "And if he'd been wrong about that, then maybe he'd been wrong about other things, too."

"My oath as a knight, he was," Devlin growled, baring his teeth. "It's no wonder you renounced your name."

"I'd never officially taken the Whitehaven name, though it was my grandmother's maiden name so I suppose I technically am one. After what I'd been through at the estate, I didn't want to use it – but I'd also long since stopped using my human surname in a bid to hide from the Hunters. I realised that we place so much weight on a name or a set of values that they become prisons, and I was tired of being an inmate. I'd never be human again and I'd never even be the type of demon that Luthier Whitehaven judged socially palatable but, in contrast, by refusing those images? I could be anyone. I could be *me*, and even if that meant spending every day of my life fighting for my next breath, nobody could take it away. So ..." she trailed off and shrugged. "I decided to just be Ivory."

"Ivory," Devlin repeated, and the way he said it sounded like a prayer. He shifted closer, his hand sliding around her waist to tug their bodies together. "I'm honoured to be trusted with your story. You are extraordinary, and if it's not too forward, I would very much like to kiss you now."

THE COST OF REDEMPTION

IF THIS WAS THE price he had to pay, Devlin swore he would pay it a thousand times over, just to see the softening in Ivory's features and the way her dark eyes shimmered with warmth. One barrier at a time, she was letting him in, this woman who'd been so terribly treated by life that her only solace was in anger, vengeance and bitterness.

"A kiss, you say?" Her lips tilted up at the corners, the guarded expression she normally wore slipping in favour of something intrinsically feminine.

"Yes," Devlin whispered, spreading the fingers of his free hand along the length of her spine. The loose sweater she wore allowed him to feel every dip and hollow, every vertebrae that was slightly more pronounced than a regular human's would be, and damn if that didn't make him want her even more. "I want to kiss you like you deserve, hot and hard and overwhelming. I want to hold you close while I—"

He broke off, body boiling and cock tight even as his heart sank. What was he saying? In order to get his hands on her, he'd have to put his head down somewhere – and if he did that, he couldn't kiss her. Frustration curdled his ardour and Devlin loosened his grip to step away.

"Wait," Ivory murmured, her voice sultry as sin. Tugging his head out of his hands, she rose on her toes and set it atop the stump of his neck. With her weight braced against his and her arms looped over his shoulders, they could have been two completely normal people sharing an intimate moment. "Now," Ivory said, so softly that he shivered, "I believe you were making some rather bold claims involving hot, hard and overwhelming?"

Unable to believe what he was hearing, Devlin tentatively slid his arms – *both* of them – around Ivory's waist, locking her body against his. When he curved his shoulders, the way she held him meant that his head dipped too, and for that wild, incredible second, he remembered what it was like to be whole.

He kissed her.

Damnation had never been so sweet as the feel of Ivory's surrender. Her lips parted under his, her body melting as his fingers dug into her skin and his tongue swept into her mouth with the fervour of a conquering army. He *needed* her and she responded in kind, lifting her legs to wrap them around his waist and growling as he slid one hand over her butt to pull her against his erection. He turned to brace her against the kitchen wall, his free hand slipping under the hem of her top to find smooth skin underneath. Ivory arched into his touch and Devlin ground against her as he explored the muscles covering her ribs, trailing his fingers upward to brush the underside of one breast.

He broke the kiss to stare down at her, glorying in the way her cheeks were flushed and her breath came in gasps. "May I—"

"You fucking better," Ivory growled, snapping her teeth in front of his nose. When Devlin still hesitated, she wriggled in his arms, somehow managing to keep his head in place and deposit her breast in his hand at the same time. "To think you were doing so well at hot, hard, and overwhelming until now."

Devlin's jaw dropped, his brain scrambled by the feel of her against his palm. "Aggression is one thing but taking liberties is quiet another."

"Taking liberties," Ivory repeated, pitching her voice high and speaking as though she had a plum stuck in her mouth. "Well, honourable knight, since you seem to be concerned: you have my unequivocal consent to do as you please until I say otherwise." Her voice dropped back into sinful territory, her hips rolling against his. "I'm no fainting damsel, Devlin. I want you pushy and wild. I want you to let go and embrace who you really are."

"But I'm a monster," Devlin groaned, resting his forehead against hers.

Ivory raised a challenging brow. "So am I."

Oh, gods, that was it. Completely undone, Devlin took her mouth again in a frenzy of teeth and tongue. Her breast was still in his hand and when he moulded her flesh with his fingers Ivory gasped, trailing kisses along the line of his jaw and down the side of his neck to nip at the edge of his collarbone. He was in the process of formulating a plan to get them both naked without his head becoming too much of a hindrance when the cottage shook, the windows vibrating in their frames and the mugs and pots hanging over the bench clattering against one another.

"The wards," Ivory gasped, levering herself up to look over Devlin's shoulder. "There are Hunters in the forest."

"At the cottage?" Though his blood thrummed with disappointment, Devlin made no protest as Ivory unhooked her legs from his waist and hurried over to the kitchen bench.

"No – I have tripwire wards bordering the edge of the forest." Setting his head down on the polished surface, she gave his nose a tweak and snatched up the pot containing the cleansing potion. "If we get this finished fast enough, we can still throw them off."

With quick, steady movements, Ivory strained the liquid through a fine gauze and tipped the solids into a mortar and pestle. Devlin cleared his throat as she began to crush them with practised movements. "I can do that, if it would speed up the process."

"It would." Flashing him a grateful smile, she pushed the pestle to the edge of the bench and rushed out of the room.

Devlin eyed his body, still facing the wall Ivory had been braced against a bare minute earlier. He'd long grown used to having his senses in two places at once, but he winced as he turned and caught sight of the bulge in the front of his trousers. Denim was certainly a marvellous invention in terms of blending durability and comfort, but it did nothing to disguise how badly he wanted Ivory naked and on top of him.

Naked, because he wanted to appreciate every glorious inch of her, and on top of him, because if he was lying on his back, Devlin was pretty sure he could pull off a reasonable imitation of an entire person while he made love to her – provided they weren't too acrobatic. He winced as he scooped the mortar and pestle against his chest. Pulling off a reasonable imitation of an entire person wasn't what he wanted and it certainly wasn't what Ivory deserved, but what more could he offer? If his curse was broken—

Devlin froze, his mouth going dry.

How could he have forgotten his curse? It was, after all, the entire reason he followed Ivory around in the first place ... and to share her bed without disclosing the true nature of it was a level of dishonour to which he would never sink.

Ivory chose that moment to rush back into the kitchen, dreadlocks wild about her face and clothes still mussed from Devlin's earlier attentions. Oblivious to the way her peeking bra strap distracted him from his task, she set a solid wooden chest on the bench, along with an empty ceramic bowl the size of her palm. Her clawed fingers were deft on the chest's clasp and a moment later she used a crude wooden spoon to scoop fine black powder into the ceramic bowl.

"Charcoal," she said, flicking him a look from beneath her

lashes. "It's what I use to make the liniments I coat my fingers in before I leave the house."

"And we need it for this ... why?"

She huffed out a breath as she poured some of the liquid from the pan into the bowl, then added a pinch of the crushed ingredients in Devlin's mortar. "Because I normally drink the solution, and it just occurred to me that you can't do that – so unless you want me to toss you to the Hunters, we'll need to get creative."

"Uh ..." Devlin cleared his throat. "When we first met, you gave the impression you'd rather walk away than help me."

"And yet, here we are." Ivory hunted through the top drawer for a smaller wooden spoon, tapping the top of Devlin's head with the handle before mixing the contents of her ceramic bowl into a sticky looking paste. "Trust me – if I wanted you gone, you'd be gone by now."

"You sound angry about that."

"I am." She laughed, even as she lifted the spoon to check the mixture's consistency. "I'm so fucking angry my teeth hurt. Letting people into my life hasn't worked well in the past, so I make a habit of not doing it in the present. Still, no matter how many times I tell myself it would be safer to kick you to the curb, here I am making you a custom cord-cutting liniment to save our hides from your ancient ex-boss and his horde of slavering zealots. Now, strip."

Devlin blinked. "I beg your pardon?"

"Strip," Ivory repeated, and when he didn't immediately respond, she set her bowl on the bench and began yanking his leather jacket off his shoulders. "I need to paint this on your skin. Bailey!"

A harrumphing snort announced Bailey's return to full wakefulness, the deathcharger crowding the bench a second later. Having successfully liberated Devlin's jacket from his body, Ivory dumped it on the floor, snatched the jug of potion off the counter and poured a generous amount back into the cooking pot.

"Drink this, my lovely." Ivory slid the pot underneath Bailey's nose. "All of it."

Bailey's ears flickered, then she shrugged and stuck her face into the pot, lapping away at the potion within.

Devlin's jaw dropped, his attention torn between the deathcharger and the way Ivory tugged his t-shirt up over his pectorals. "How did you do that?"

"Do what? Fuck's sake, Devlin, help me out here," Ivory growled, poking him sharply in the gut with a claw.

Devlin jumped, but obligingly raised his arms so that she could pull his t-shirt off and toss it across the room.

"How did you get Bailey to drink without protest? She wouldn't do that for me, no matter how nicely I asked."

"I'm prettier than you."

Her fingers tugged at his belt, and it was half undone by the time Devlin caught her wrists. "No."

Ivory glanced over her shoulder to meet his eyes. "Yes. I need to paint this on your skin, Devlin, and we don't have time to worry about that awkward birthmark you'd rather I not see. Now let me take your fucking pants off, or I'll shred them."

"I don't have an awkward birthmark," Devlin muttered, releasing her grip on his wrists.

Watching Ivory unzip his jeans and tug them down his legs, leaving him in nothing but the snug cotton undergarments he'd attained in the clothing store, was nothing short of torture. He tried to imagine how it would look if his head was on top of his body rather than viewing proceedings from the middle of the bench, and couldn't – it had been too long since he'd had that viewpoint on a regular basis. But this way ... he could see every single one of his ridged muscles, marred by the patchwork of scars he'd earned over the course of his life as a knight; and he could see the slim, curvy form of Ivory as she knelt at his feet, her face devastatingly close to the insistent bulge in his underwear.

"Left foot," she commanded, and Devlin braced one hand on

her shoulder as she tugged off his boot and sock, then his jeans. "Right foot."

After shoving his clothes and boots aside, Ivory rose onto her knees, fingers trailing up the outside of his thighs. Devlin's breath hitched as she settled her palms on his hipbones and flicked a cheeky look over one shoulder. When their eyes met, she winked. "Come on now, big boy, it's not so bad, is it?"

No. Yes. Noyesno. Devlin opened his mouth to respond when she turned back to face his cock and rubbed her cheek against it like a kitten seeking affection. The contact was akin to being struck by lightning and he clenched his fists lest he make a mess all over the place – only his fists somehow ended up in Ivory's hair, the side of her face pressed firmly to his crotch.

She laughed, the sound vibrating through his body and making him whimper. Gently disentangling his fingers from her hair, she stood, scooping his head up in one hand and the ceramic bowl in the other. With soft words and a gentle push, she coaxed his body into the loungeroom and bade him stretch out on the bare wooden floor behind the couch.

"If you're a good knight, you'll get a treat once this is done," she told him, carefully positioning his head atop his neck where it was, biologically speaking, meant to be. "But for now, we have to keep you safe."

"What about you?" Devlin croaked, so far out of his depth that he gave up trying to swim and just let the current sweep him away. "You need to be safe, too."

"Here," Bailey whickered. Ivory turned to accept the jug clenched carefully in the deathcharger's pointed teeth and smiled.

"Thank you." She patted Bailey's jaw, set the jug to her lips and began to swallow, not bothering to stop for breath until the potion was almost entirely gone. Setting the jug on the floor out of the way, she raised a brow at Devlin. "Satisfied?"

"No," he croaked, and she laughed again.

"Hold tight, now." Ivory dipped her fingers into the ceramic bowl. "This might tickle."

It was very difficult to remember that they were in danger as Ivory began to draw on his chest. Her eyes were only partially focussed, as though she listened to a voice only she could hear while strange characters began to take shape on the surface of Devlin's skin. Once his chest was covered in what he now vaguely recognised as demonic runes, she spread liniment on his cheeks, then his forehead, before returning to his torso and working her way down his abs, then his thighs, shins, and even the tops of his feet. Everywhere she touched was like fire but Devlin couldn't decide if it was the liniment or Ivory herself, and the inherent enchantment engendered by her proximity. When she returned to his shoulders, fingers skimming lightly down his arms to draw on his biceps, Devlin let out an involuntary groan.

"Almost there." Ivory drew the last few runes on the backs of his hands then shot Devlin a hot look from beneath her lashes. "Ready?"

"For wh – aaaah!" Devlin arched off the floor as Ivory leant down and licked his abdomen, her tongue trailing across the leading edge of one of the runes she'd drawn. It immediately began to glow, a tingling heat sweeping across his skin as the rest of the characters activated. Crawling up his body with a sinful grin on her face, Ivory licked one of the characters on his cheek, nipped the tip of his nose and then, laughing when his arms banded tight around her waist, pressed her lips against his. She tasted of charcoal and magic and woman, and Devlin let the kiss carry him away even though he knew he shouldn't.

Ivory drew back with a soft chuckle. "There; all better."

"Are we ..." Devlin cleared his throat, tried again. "Cleansed?"

"Yes." Ivory's eyes unfocused, her brow furrowing. "They haven't tripped any of the inner forest alarms, so I'd wager that once the cleansing ritual settles, the Hunters will move on fairly quickly. You'll be free to go by nightfall."

Devlin swallowed. "You helped Bailey and I, even when you didn't want to. I'd like to repay your kindness."

Ivory raised an eyebrow, lips twitching into a very naughty smile.

"Not like that," Devlin grumbled, catching her hand when it started to slide south. "I mean, yes, I want to do that, but it's not a form of currency and I wouldn't dream of sharing your bed—"

"Or the lounge room floor?"

"—or the lounge room floor, or anywhere for that matter, without being completely honest with you."

She tilted her head to the side. "Your demonic semen is like acid, and will melt my insides?"

"What?" Devlin spluttered and coughed, releasing his grip on her waist to wave his hands in the negative. "No, no! I mean ..." he sighed. "You have to promise to hear me out."

Ivory's smile faded and her eyes narrowed. "This is about the curse I'm not breaking, isn't it?"

Damn, but he wished he could nod his head. Instead, Devlin settled for chewing on his bottom lip. "Yes."

"For the love of – all right. I'll listen, and we can consider it part of whatever payment you think you owe." Pulling out of his grip, Ivory assumed a cross-legged position by his right shoulder and folded both arms over her chest. "Talk."

"Can I get dressed first?"

"No."

Devlin growled, but in the end, what did it matter? It had taken him all this time to simply get Ivory to listen – he wasn't about to throw that opportunity away for the comfort of a pair of pants.

"All right. My curse needs to be broken on Halloween."

One dark brow shot up. "Cliché. Also, Halloween's in ... what? Two days?"

"It's not meant to be cliché, just the truth. What little I've discovered over the centuries dictates that the curse of a demon who has died is very tricky to break. It requires someone on this side of the veil with the right power – in this case, you – and it requires the spirit of the demon on the other side to give his or her permission. The sort of energy harmonising for that kind of co-operation is only possible on the night when the veil between all the worlds is thinnest."

"Halloween." Ivory nodded, her mouth twisting to the side. "Yes, I suppose that makes sense. Travelling between Earth and Mu is one thing, but you're talking about the afterlife; even I know that calls for more juice." Her eyes narrowed. "I'm not sure what this has to do with me, though."

"When the curse is broken, the demonic power trapped inside me will be transferred to whoever broke it. In this case, you." Devlin brushed a hand over her knee, revelling in the warmth of her skin beneath his touch. "I don't know much about demonic magic but I can tell you this with certainty: the woman I killed was able to assume a human form. If her magic passed to you ..."

Ivory gasped. "I'd be able to assume a human form."
"Yes."

"I ... I'd look normal." Ivory extended her hands, staring down at her too-pale skin and clawed fingers, several of which were stained black with liniment. "I'd be able to walk down the street without people hissing or cursing or throwing things at me. I could visit a park, or open a potion shop, or stop to admire the sunset." She swallowed heavily. "I could hide from the Hunters."
"Yes."

A long, tense minute passed, and then Ivory smacked him in the shoulder. "Why didn't you tell me this to begin with? It changes everything!"

"You said you weren't interested," Devlin replied with a shrug. "I may no longer be a knight by technicality, but I'm not an asshole. When a lady says no, she means no."
"I ..."

"A lady also reserves the right to change her mind," Devlin added, hope swirling in his chest. "I made a terrible mistake a long time ago and I want to pay my debt. I can no longer help the woman whose life I stole, but I can help you." He wiggled sideways, putting his body out of alignment with his head but managing to snare her fingers with his own. "Let me atone for my sins. Let me give you this gift."

Ivory stared down at their joined fingers, her eyes glistening with moisture. She swallowed, shook her head, swallowed again. "I ..."

"Please," Devlin whispered, squeezing her hand.

At long last she looked up, their gazes colliding with enough force that had he been a breather, he'd have stopped in that one moment. Ivory took a breath deep enough for both of them, her fingers so tight around Devlin's that her claws dug into the back of his knuckles – but when she spoke, her voice was steady.

"All right, Devlin. I'll do it. I'll break your curse."

THERE'S ALWAYS A CATCH

NORMAL. SHE COULD BE NORMAL.

The word rang in Ivory's head like the reverberation from a gong, echoing inside her skull until she moved as though in a dream. She vaguely remembered clearing away the trail-cleansing potion and gathering Devlin's clothes before showing him to the bathroom where he could safely shower the liniment off his oh-so-lickable skin. He didn't ask her to join him and Ivory didn't so much as glance in the direction of his tight ass as she left him to his ablutions.

Could she go to school? Completing formal schooling had never seemed a priority when it was out of reach but now ...

Ivory shook her head in wonder as she opened the door to the basement. Would she *need* to finish her basic schooling? Or, since she could read and write already, would she be able to take a business management course right off the bat? Throat thickening, she paused at the base of the worn wooden stairs.

She could open a shop. She could sell potions and liniments and poultices and teas and spices and books. She could smile at people with normal teeth, rather than a mouth full of pointed predator chompers. She could wear headbands in her hair, because her horns wouldn't be there to get in the way. She could get a manicure at a human beauty salon because she would *look like a human.* Nobody would scream or swear. Nobody would throw things at her, or hit her, or accuse her of being a foul, pestilential creature intent on sodomising Grandma with her barbed tail.

She didn't even *have* a tail.

Ivory cut off her thoughts with a strangled laugh, shoved open the door to the library and moved inside. Due to a clever arrangement of vents and mirrors, the room was filled with ambient light and in the evening, Lemurian crystals suffused the library in a soft glow so it was never in true darkness. Not like the first night Ivory had spent here, frightened and hungry and alone, so desperate for contact that she imagined the voices of her ancestors – contained in the myriad journals lining the library's crude wooden shelves – were talking to her.

Of course, they *were* talking to her; when Ivory read the books, the echo of the author was a constant whisper in her ear. It had taken a lot of reading, ruminating and several epiphanies to realise that was part of her magic, the wondrous, different, not-at-all-missing magic that had been passed down via generations of women with demonic blood.

A book snagged her attention and she smiled as she drew the slim volume from the shelves. What would Jacinta say when Ivory turned up on her doorstep looking normal? They could have tea by the shop's front desk without worrying about scaring the customers, and they could chat about Ivory's proposal to offer goods at wholesale prices in return for references to her own store.

Grinning in anticipation, Ivory settled into a nearby armchair, allowing the book in her hands to drop open where it willed. Once the pages had settled, she took a deep breath, called her chaotic thoughts to order and began to read.

Mother's soul cries out in torment. My ability to

connect across the veil grows weaker every day, no matter the circles I cast nor the symbols I evoke, but I'm certain the transfer was arrested somehow and she cannot cross over. The implication that He Who Was Cursed would be able to disrupt the process is staggering; only an event of catastrophic proportions would be strong enough to halt the transition. And, I cannot help but wonder, to what purpose? In this half form, He will be neither alive nor dead, human nor demon, his soul tied to Mother's in an eternal, soul-wrenching twist. If only Father would tell me where He hides, I would seek him myself and endeavour to break the cycle so Mother could rest - but Father is notoriously tight-lipped on the subject. I wonder, if he could hear her pain, would he still feel the same?

Ivory blinked, frowning, and read the passage again. She was in the midst of her third read-through when someone cleared their throat; she looked up to see Devlin at the end of the aisle.

He really was handsome. The more time Ivory spent with him, the less she noticed that his head was detached from his body and the more she was drawn to the sheer masculinity of his presence; tall and broad and so very delicious. Built like a knight was fabled to be, with muscles earned from swinging his sword and that misguided sense of justice and honour which should have irritated her, but that she somehow found charming. His infernal green eyes glowed faintly, a sure sign of demonic blood – and yet they were not as bright as Bailey's, nor his blood as dark as it should be.

"You never completed the transition to full demon." It wasn't a question, because the clues had been there all along. "You stopped the process somehow."

An odd, not-quite smile tugged at his lips. "Decapitation."

"What?"

Devlin sighed, shoulders sagging as though under a great weight. After a few moments' silence, he crossed to the armchair and sank to the floor beside it, resting his head on one bent knee.

"After I killed your ancestor, I spent several days in the forest with a fever and only Bailey to nurse me. Between the horrid aches and hallucinations, I realised the curse was turning me *into* a demon." Devlin's lips thinned. "Back then, I believed as my knightly brethren did: that demons were an unholy blight to be cleansed from the world. I did not wish to contribute to the number of demons needing to be ... removed, so I decided to remove myself. I returned to Gawain in the dark of night and begged him to help me."

"So he cut off your head?"

Devlin's eyes glinted with macabre amusement. "Different demons require killing in different ways, but we had yet to come across one who could survive without their head attached to their body – so, yes, we agreed that decapitation was the best way to solve the problem." His lips thinned. "I knelt at Gawain's feet and bent my head. I said my knightly funerary rites and my farewells. Gawain wept, but his hand was firm on his sword, and he promised to remember me when I was gone. Then, as you said, he cut off my head."

Ivory inspected the stump, then lowered her eyes to Devlin's. "He did a neat job."

Laughter echoed through the library and Ivory smiled in spite of herself, disarmed by the easy way he'd shared such a traumatic memory.

"My first inkling that something wasn't right was when I opened my eyes, sat up, and spied a set of headless shoulders. It took me several minutes to work out that I was seeing my own body from the angle of my severed head." His brow furrowed.

"There must have been a period of disconnect, because I was no longer in Gawain's room but laid out on a funerary bier in one of our churches. I panicked, snatched up my head and ran into the night – and Bailey was there, only her eyes glowed and she was no longer the Bailey I'd known before but this newer, smarter, demonic Bailey. When she lowered to her knees, I fell across her back in a most un-knightly fashion and dropped my head on the ground." He snorted a dry laugh. "Bailey carried my head in her mouth by clenching her teeth in my hair – and I have never been so grateful to have put off cutting it as I was then, I can assure you."

"Wait. You were decapitated by your friend, woke up in an open casket, your destrier had turned into a deathcharger ... and you were worried about the length of your *hair?*" Ivory shoved a fist into her mouth to contain her laugh. "That's ridiculous."

Devlin grinned. "It's the little things, I suppose, when you're stressed."

She sobered at that and nodded. "It is indeed."

"I don't know why I didn't die," Devlin said quietly. "I've asked that question so many times over the thousands of years that followed, but I have never found the answer."

"A glitch in the magic, perhaps." Ivory drummed her fingers on the book in her lap and then, after a moment's indecision, read out the passage she'd found before his arrival.

Devlin's eyebrows shot up. "You think this pertains to me?"

"Definitely." Ivory gestured at the stone and earth walls. "The library, like the cottage and the grounds, is saturated with the echoes of my ancestors. Whenever I come down here with a question, the shelves give me whatever book I need to find the answer."

Rather than look pleased, Devlin's shoulders hunched. "I stole a mother from her children." His eyes squeezed shut. "I stole a wife from her husband, a woman from her life, all because of my own arrogance and bigotry – and if this passage is correct, she has suffered for every moment I have endured in this

71

wretched half state." Long lashes lifted, green eyes burning bright with determination. "It is well past time I set her free."

Ivory ran a hand over the book's worn cover. It had been years since she'd needed kind words and they came rusty off her tongue, her voice stiff. "We'll find a way. I promise."

As her fingers lifted from the journal, a frisson went through the pages. The slim volume bounced off Ivory's lap and tumbled to the floor, falling open at a short entry towards the back. Rather than pick it up, she slid off the chair and onto her knees, hunching over to read aloud.

"*Father has taken the location of He Who Was Cursed to his grave. I have heard rumours, however; a Headless Horseman who haunts his hollow and speaks only in shrieks and grunts. I'm convinced he's the one, yet none can tell me where this cursed hollow lies. I refuse to be deterred, for if I can connect this Headless Horseman with Mother's spirit, together they can untangle this mess – and the Cursed One will either accept her power to become whole, or pass it on to her nearest living descendant and resign himself to his fate. At this point, I care not which, so long as it puts Mother's soul to rest. With Father gone and Dindella happily married, there is nothing to keep me here: tomorrow I will begin the search for this cursed hollow and the Headless One who resides there, and perhaps, together, we can end this tragedy. I can only pray that he will listen, should I be lucky enough to find him.*"

She glanced up at Devlin and he shrugged. "Nobody ever came to my hollow claiming to know who I was, or how to end the curse."

"Hmm." Ivory flipped the last few pages, but they were blank. She stopped at the back cover and made a face. "There's a note here, presumably from the sister, that says Gloraya died about a month after the final entry was written."

"She dedicated her life to ending her mother's torment," Devlin said miserably. "If I were able to leave the hollow sooner, perhaps I'd have been able to go to her, rather than have her die trying to find me."

"You couldn't leave the hollow?"

"No." His brow furrowed. "There was a clear demarcation which I could not cross, though others could come in. It disappeared a few years ago when, as far as I've been able to piece together, the two worlds were reunited."

"You mean when they merged."

"No – they were partially merged already," Devlin corrected. "I was human, but I worked often with those who had mixed blood, and full Lemurians too. Gawain, for example, is a full-blooded fae; I have also dealt with angels, vampires, centaurs ... what? Why are you looking at me like that?"

"Because you're talking about a time before written history – a time when Atlantis existed and technology was far more advanced than anything humanity has been able to accomplish thus far." Ivory blew out a sharp breath. "You're ... Devlin, you're talking about ..."

"I suppose I'm older than I care to think," he admitted ruefully. "Yes, I hail from a time so long in the past that it's been buried deep – until the gods returned, of course, and set everything to rights."

Since she was a by-product of that return, Ivory snorted at the word 'rights' – but rather than rail at a fate she couldn't change, she pursed her lips and thought back on Devlin's story. "I think I know what went wrong."

"Oh?"

"If the worlds were partially merged, then there must have been magic back then, right?"

He blinked. "Of course; though on Earth, it was limited to those few sites where the Merge had already taken hold. I served Gawain and the Knights of the Round Table in a small kingdom that was the gateway between Earth and the fae realm of Camelot."

"Camelot," Ivory choked, shaking her head. "Fairytales aside, the first journal entry said that Gloraya's ability to connect across the veil was weakening. We already know, from what the gods have revealed, that there was a barrier erected between the two worlds that cut off magic until the Earth was strong enough to bear the load."

"Was there?" Devlin's eyes rounded in amazement.

"Yes. What if that happened around the time of your cursing and decapitation? A surge in magic like that would be more than enough to interrupt not only the transition process and your death, but it could also bind you and Bailey to the hollow – where I'm assuming there was some sort of magical resonance that remained after the barrier was erected."

"And once the barrier came down and the worlds were truly Merged, that restriction eased and I was able to leave." Devlin whistled between his teeth. "It's possible. It's very, very possible."

"It also means we should have no trouble reaching through the veil once Halloween hits." Ivory frowned. "The only thing I don't understand is the choice that was referenced in the journal."

Devlin shifted against the wall, readjusting his head where it sat on his leg. "It is of little matter. As long as you connect me to your ancestor, I can pass the powers to you and pay my debt."

"Pay your debt," Ivory repeated. Her eyes narrowed, an odd, prickly feeling curdling her stomach. "You've said that a few times now. What does it mean, exactly?"

He chewed on his lower lip and said nothing.

... the Cursed One will either accept her power to become whole, or pass it on to her nearest living descendant and resign himself to his fate ...

"You could choose to keep the power," she whispered, watching Devlin from beneath her lashes. "The magic would restore your head to your shoulders and complete the transition to full demon."

"I didn't know I could complete the rite and be restored, but that matters little; I promised the power to you, and I keep my word."

"Okay, so let's say you give the power to me, and I gain the ability to assume a human form, like we discussed." Ivory swallowed. "Then what happens?"

"I pay my debt."

"How, Devlin?" Her voice rose, her muscles tightening until it seemed they might snap. "How do you pay?"

Devlin sighed, directing his gaze over her shoulder, and for a moment Ivory thought she would have to beat the answer out of him – until he looked back at her with such intensity in his expression that it felt like a physical blow.

"Passing the power to you would revert me to my original state. I'd become fully human again," he said quietly.

"But ... without your head ..."

"I'd die." Devlin's eyes crinkled slightly at the corners, his smile one of gentle acceptance. It was simultaneously the most hideously pious and heartbreakingly beautiful thing Ivory had ever seen. "A life for a life. That is how I pay my debt."

THE ILLUSION OF HONOUR

IT HAD BEEN THE right thing to do.

At least, that's what Devlin told himself, curled up that night against Bailey's flank. She slept soundly, her soft breathing comforting as he stared out Ivory's lounge room window at the stars that burned brightly overhead.

It had been the right thing to do.

Even if Ivory's face had twisted in horror at his words; even if she'd thrown him out of the house, screaming obscenities all the while. Even if, when she'd let him back in as the sun set, the passion they'd ignited in the kitchen was nothing but ashes. After all this time, after all the suffering he'd caused, honour was all Devlin had left. He'd pay the debt he owed – to Ivory, to the nameless woman whose life he'd stolen, to her husband and her two daughters – because it was the right thing to do.

It was too bad that pointing that out to Ivory had gotten him stabbed in the thigh with a fork.

Devlin brushed a hand over the site of the wound. The punctures had long since disappeared, but a residual ache lingered – though this one, curiously enough, was in his chest instead of his leg. It pulsed in mockery of the heartbeat he no longer had, every passing moment cementing the impossible wish that he could pay his debts and somehow, some way, still chase the fragile thing which connected him to Ivory.

When the soft breath of dawn began to creep through the cottage and her bedroom door creaked open, the ache intensified to such a degree that Devlin rubbed a hand over his sternum. There wasn't enough light to do more than glimpse a sleepy face surrounded by a thick fall of black dreadlocks, the silver ring in Ivory's nose glinting as she moved to set the kettle on the stove.

Devlin sighed. He'd come here chasing peace and forgiveness, and now he craved another second, another minute, another day – however long he could cajole, just to stay close to the woman in the next room.

Damn.

"Halloween is tomorrow." Ivory began scooping a variety of reagents into a small pot, studiously avoiding Devlin's gaze. "Contrary to popular opinion, we won't need midnight to reach across the veil; any time of the day will do."

"You ... you're still going through with it?"

She paused, knuckles white around a jar of star anise. "I don't want to, Devlin. I don't want your powers at the cost of your life. But ... I also can't leave my ancestor tethered to you indefinitely; not if it's causing her pain. So, yeah, I'm still going through with it." Ivory cleared her throat and went back to scooping, though her hands trembled as she did. "I'll be spending today gathering things for the ritual."

"I'll help you," Devlin said at once, sitting up so quickly his head tumbled off his lap and rolled face down on the rug.

"Yes, you will," Ivory agreed, her wooden spoon clanging against the pot while Devlin patted the area around him in search of his wayward head. "We'll be leaving in an hour ... oh, for fuck's sake."

Skin whispered over hardwood floors and then clawed fingers clenched none too gently in his hair. Devlin had the barest glimpse of tattered sleep pants before his head was dropped unceremoniously into his lap and Ivory stalked back into the kitchen.

"Thanks," Devlin muttered, righting his head on his knee so he could watch her continue to brew the tea. "What do you need?"

A short laugh echoed from the kitchen and she turned away, thumping and crashing things over by the stove. "What do I *need?* I need for people I care about not to leave at the drop of a hat. What I'm getting, however, is a blithering idiot who expects me to help him murder himself and be grateful for it."

Devlin's mouth dropped open, and he could only stare as Ivory stormed around the bench and set a bowl of oatmeal in front of Bailey. The deathcharger whickered and Ivory's face softened momentarily as she brushed Bailey's forelock back from her face.

"It's not like that," Devlin managed. Something in his gut turned cold and slippery, and he swallowed against the lump in his throat when neither horse nor woman answered. "I don't ... I don't want to ..."

Moving in perfect unison, Ivory and Bailey turned their heads, pinning him with matching glares.

"You don't want to die? Really?" Ivory's eyes blazed with fury. "Then why aren't you fighting?"

"Fighting for *what?*" He slapped a hand against his chest. "Have you stopped for a second to think that this might be beyond my control?"

Bailey's brow furrowed, and Ivory blinked. "What do you mean?"

"I'm not the one who laid the curse; I'm not the one who must choose to lift it. Do you honestly think, when I come face to face with your ancestor, that she's going to just *forgive me?*" He let out a brittle laugh. "You're acting as though I'm walking away from a second chance, but Ivory, she might not give me one. She might demand I lay down my life and return your family's power to where it rightfully belongs. Then what?"

The silence crackled with tension, but after a long moment, Bailey sighed and dropped her glare. Ivory tsked in the back of her throat and then she, too, looked away.

Devlin forced his voice to remain even. "If you're asking if I want to leave Bailey to an uncertain fate, to walk away from – light save me – from you, then the answer is no. I don't. But you said it yourself; we can't leave your ancestor tethered to me indefinitely, not if it's causing her pain." He curled his hands to fists. "This is the right thing to do."

"I hate doing the right thing." Ivory bared her teeth at him. "And right now, I hate you too."

Devlin choked, searching desperately for a reasonable response, but Ivory walked into the bathroom and slammed the door behind her.

"Dammit." He looked over at Bailey, who watched him with sad eyes. "What now?"

The deathcharger gave a sad little sigh, rolled her shoulders and began to eat her oats – because at the end of the day, no matter how they all felt, there was no other choice.

It was the right thing to do.

Once Ivory reappeared, she announced their first stop to be a human supermarket. She covered her fingers in liniments from a variety of different jars, issued a clipped warning to be alert for Hunters at all times, then withdrew into the depths of a black coat whose hood was so enormously oversized it not only hid her horns but wreathed her entire face in shadows.

She didn't speak, and neither did Devlin.

Bailey took them into town, waiting outside while Devlin followed Ivory up and down the supermarket's many aisles, dutifully holding the shopping basket and trying not to make any sudden movements that might dislodge his head from his shoulders ... even though Ivory had strapped it in place with several layers of a thick silver tape which was, for some odd reason, named after ducks.

When they reached the register, Ivory unloaded the contents

of the basket without so much as glancing in Devlin's direction. She fumbled the tin of pineapple slices and they both bent to catch it, colliding with enough force that the duck tape gave way in a spectacular ripping of adhesive. Devlin's head thunked onto the black conveyor belt, bounced off a bottle of soda water and rolled to a stop face up in front of the clerk.

"Damn," he said.

The elderly woman, wearing a grocer's smock and a name tag that read 'Senior Staff: Una,' stared at him with wide eyes.

"I'm terribly sorry," Devlin said. "I really don't think duck tape was the best choice. Perhaps you can recommend something stronger?"

Una screamed, tripping over her own feet in her haste to back away from the register. Devlin winced as her distress garnered the attention of the other people in the supermarket and one scream became two, then three, then a chorus – until, in less than a minute, the store emptied of everyone save Devlin and Ivory.

"Perhaps you can recommend something stronger?" Ivory repeated. Laughter shook her shoulders, and from his vantage point at her waist height, Devlin could just see her biting her lip to contain her mirth. "You know how to joke after all."

"I wasn't joking," Devlin grumbled, though warmth unfurled in his chest. "This duck tape is worse than the kinesiology tape I had in the RV."

Ivory coughed, the sound dissolving into a hearty laugh. "It's duct tape, you idiot. For fixing ducts. And for the record, the tape worked out exactly as I'd hoped."

"You ..." Devlin gasped. "You *meant* for my head to fall off?"

"How else am I supposed to get the groceries for free?"

"Free? They're not free! You have to pay for them!"

She shrugged and winked. "Bit difficult to pay if there's nobody here."

And before he could protest, Ivory scooped his head into the nearest shopping bag, hung the handles over her outstretched arm and tugged him out of the store. Bailey snorted the moment she saw them, and Devlin didn't need to remove his face from the bag of oranges to know she laughed at him rather than with him. Relief thumped in his blood, demanding he laugh and cry and beg their forgiveness, but since the awful tension that had reigned since dawn was only just beginning to lift, he did his best to look unimpressed instead, muttering under his breath while Ivory removed the failed duck – *duct* – tape, and then resecured his head to his neck with a fresh batch.

"There." Ivory adjusted his scarf and the neck of his leather jacket. "Fixed."

"Thank you." Devlin cleared his throat, trying not to blush. "Though I feel I should point out that my head is a little off-centre."

Ivory raised a brow, lips twitching with the barest hint of a smile. "I wouldn't worry. It's not staying on long."

It didn't. In the homewares store, Ivory let out an enormous fake sneeze, jostling Devlin so that his head toppled into a basket of plastic flowers – and once the customers had fled, she propped his head atop her loot, took his wrist and led him back out to a still-laughing Bailey.

"This is the easiest shopping I've ever done," Ivory said, rear-ranging the contents of the trolley so that the perishables wouldn't get crushed. "Talk about jumping the queue."

Devlin picked at the tape stuck to his chin. "I'm not sure if I'm supposed to approve of theft, but this is the first time anyone's appreciated the fact that my head falls off so easily."

"You're telling me you've never walked out with free stuff after your head fell off?" Ivory raised both her eyebrows. "Because if you do, I'll call you a liar."

"Oh, no – Bailey and I do that all the time. I mean, I try to pay, but it becomes difficult when everyone runs away." He frowned. "Does this make me a bad person?"

"You're asking *me*?" Ivory tilted her head, eyes dancing. "I'm morally ambiguous, remember?"

"Of course." Devlin huffed a laugh as he pulled out the roll of duct tape. "I'm not sure how this is meant to keep us from being noticed by the Hunters, though."

"It's not." Ivory screwed her face up. "One of those goody-two-shoes we scared off is probably flapping their gums even as we speak."

"But… but… *you* were the one who said we had to watch out for them!"

Ivory took the roll of tape from him with gentle fingers. "Devlin, look at me. I have horns. And claws. How long do you think it would be before someone noticed?" Her smile was soft and sad. "I can tell you – not long. Making a scene means the Hunters will still come, but they'll come where we *want* them to come; and by the time they arrive, we'll be gone."

"Oh." He lifted his hair out of the way as she began winding tape around his neck. "That makes sense, I guess. Where next?"

She grinned, and he felt like the sun had just come out. "The hardware store."

Where Ivory gave up all pretence of an accident and hit him with a thick piece of doweling, punting his head halfway across the shop to land with a splash in the ornamental fish tank behind the front counter. As he sank to rest chin-first on the pink gravel at the bottom of the tank, a miniature shark nipping at his nose, Devlin closed his eyes and let Ivory's water-distorted laughter wash over him.

All his life, he'd clung to the morals and manners that his brethren had taught him. He'd believed in justice, and honour, and honesty. Courage, benevolence, loyalty – all the tenets of a strong, righteous knight. Now, though?

Maybe Ivory was right. Maybe it was all just an illusion, because he didn't want to do what honour demanded. He didn't want to leave.

He didn't want to do the right thing.

Soaking up the odd peace that came from being underwater with one's face pressed against a plastic pirate ship, Devlin sighed. His mission had started simply enough; now it involved a demon caring about a headless ex-knight who carried a sword the colour of old blood and rode a destrier-turned-deathcharger. Just as he cared about her, far more than he should for the short time they'd known one another, far more than was reasonable or logical or ... human.

The little shark had begun to nudge the end of Devlin's left eyebrow by the time Ivory's hand plunged into the tank, streams of darkness trailing from her clawed fingers. She cradled the back of his head and brought him to the surface nose-first, like a sunken wreck being salvaged from the very depths of the ocean.

"I'm sorry," Devlin said, the moment his lips were back in the open air.

Ivory paused, and for a moment, he wondered if she was going to drop him back into the tank. "I know."

"I don't know how to fix this," he admitted. "What I broke."

"You do," she responded, her breath catching unsteadily. "And so do I. It's why we're going through with this, in spite of how we feel about it." Her brows furrowed. "But if you tell anyone I'm doing what might be considered the right thing, I will find a way to end you."

Devlin blinked water from his eyes and offered his most charming smile. "I'll be sure to enjoy every minute."

Ivory's mouth dropped open, revealing every single one of her pointed demonic teeth. She stared at him wide-eyed for almost two entire minutes before she shook her head, yanked him the rest of the way out of the tank, and stalked out of the store with her brows furrowed into a frown.

She drew up on the footpath, shoving his head back against his chest so she could fist both hands on her hips. "What happens to Bailey when you die?"

"What?"

"Assuming it all goes wrong tomorrow, and you don't get a choice. If you die, does Bailey die? Is her demonic state connected to yours?"

"I don't think so." Devlin glanced towards where the deathcharger stood guard a few paces away. "She made the full transition when I did not. If my choice is made for me, and I don't return tomorrow, then ... well, I assumed she would simply stay with whoever had broken my curse. So ... you."

Ivory crinkled her nose. "Leaving me to clean up your mess without even asking first? What a guy."

"It's not like that," Devlin protested, his throat inexplicably thick. "I just ..."

"I know." She closed her eyes, and for a moment the three of them stood in tortured silence. "We better get out of here before the Hunters catch wind of us."

"Yes." Devlin followed as she stalked away, hips swaying and the heels of her boots clicking furiously on the pavement. "How much time do we have?"

"No idea, but it'll happen eventually. It always does." Pulling up in front of a vehicle with a large tub at the back, Ivory licked the tip of one claw and stuck it into the locking mechanism. The metal hissed and sagged, silver alloy dripping onto the road until the vehicle issued a sad beep and the door unlocked.

The clatter of hooves announced the arrival of Bailey, her mouth fastened over the handle of the trolley so that she could drag it along behind her. Balancing his head on the side of the vehicle, Devlin unlatched the back and began transferring the many bags and boxes that Ivory had acquired while Bailey curled up in the tub, her enormous bulk squashed against the vehicle's edges and the suspension groaning in protest.

Devlin shut the tailgate as the engine rumbled to life, the vehicle vibrating beneath him. After a moment's hesitation, he spread his fingers across the deathcharger's shoulder. "Is there not honour in repenting my mistakes?"

Bailey considered him a long moment, pale green eyes flickering with infernal light. "Yes."

"Then why does it hurt more than I ever thought possible?"
Bailey's expression softened. "Heart."

"I suppose you're right. If I didn't care, it wouldn't hurt, and if it didn't hurt, it wouldn't be penance." Devlin blew out a long breath. "I never expected the cost to be so steep."

"Hmph." Bailey tipped her head to the side. "Paid already."

Devlin frowned. "You think the time I spent bound to the hollow is payment enough?"

"Yes."

"All we can do is hope my ancestor agrees." Ivory appeared on the opposite side of the vehicle, where she reached to run her fingers through Bailey's mane. "I hate hope."

"I think, perhaps, that I do, too." Devlin gripped the side of the vehicle so hard the metal groaned in protest. "I don't want to leave Bailey."

I don't want to leave you.

"Sad," Bailey whickered.

"I know, gorgeous. I know. But what other choice do we have?" Ivory spat on the pavement. It sizzled. "It's the right thing to do."

ALL HALLOW'S EVE

IVORY LAY IN BED until the morning sun peeked through the gap between her curtains, cutting a ray of brilliance across the heavy gloom. Sleep – or lack thereof – had her eyes full of sand and her brain full of wool, and for reasons she absolutely refused to examine, her breathing was truncated and her heart hurt with every rhythmic beat.

Halloween was here.

Perhaps she should've given in to her cravings the previous night and invited Devlin to bed. She knew he'd have come; his interest in her was no secret, after all. And yet ... it was precisely because she wanted him that she'd left him in the lounge room.

Letting out a heavy sigh, Ivory rubbed both hands over her face. Logically, she hadn't known Devlin long enough to feel the depth of emotion that she did. She wasn't a creature of logic, however, she was a demon, and demons burned hot and bright. Sometimes so bright they were consumed by their passions and turned terribly evil.

Ivory lifted a hand and stared at her pale skin, the long, curved claws that marked her as anything but human. Not so long ago, she'd rejoiced at the idea of assuming a human form

86

but now, knowing it meant Devlin's destruction ... she didn't want to give him up.

For once, just once, she wanted someone to choose *her*. She wanted to be enough to fill someone so full that they overflowed with it, that they'd embrace a culture they'd once sworn to destroy. She wanted to be loved.

No.

She wanted to be loved by *Devlin*.

A soft knock sounded at the bedroom door and Ivory rose, opening it to find not Devlin, as she'd expected, but Bailey. The deathcharger looked ludicrous crammed in the small doorway, her shoulders pushing against the frame and smoke curling from her nostrils but rather than comment, Ivory looped her arms around Bailey's neck and buried her face in lengths of long, silky black mane.

"Where is he?" Ivory whispered.

"Washing."

Ivory focussed her attention on the background noise of the cottage and registered the sound of the shower running. She squeezed Bailey a little tighter. "We'll be okay. If ... if things don't go the way we hope, you can stay with me and we'll spend the rest of our years bitter and jaded together. I promise."

The deathcharger sighed as she tucked her head around Ivory in the equine equivalent of a hug. "Yes."

"Gods and demons, this is stupid," Ivory muttered, her eyes stinging. "So, so stupid."

"Yes," Bailey snorted, her chest rumbling with a laugh. "Stupid."

Ivory laughed too, wobbly though it was, and they stood in silence until the shower cut off and Devlin could be heard grumbling to himself as he tried to manage his head and his towel at the same time.

"Well." Ivory stepped back and wiped her eyes. "I guess that means it's my turn, and then ... we get this done."

Bailey nodded, and by the time Devlin emerged, Ivory had

packed everything she was going to need into an old-fashioned picnic basket. After a quick shower, she dressed in comfortable jeans and a long-line sweater that clung to her curves and was, in keeping with her mood, a dark grey.

"Ready?" She flicked Devlin a glance, noting he wore the same outfit he'd had on since they'd met. "No clean clothes?"

"They were in the RV." He shrugged, looking uncomfortable. "I didn't mention anything yesterday because ..."

"Right. Fair enough." Pressing her lips together, Ivory snatched up the basket and made for the door. "Let's go, then."

"Wait." Devlin made as if to reach for her, pulling up short at the last moment. "The Hunters have to have worked out we're in this area by now. Is it safe?"

Ivory blew out a long breath. "The Hunters have been chasing me for years, Devlin. Every time I leave the wards, there's a chance that either they'll find me, or someone will tell them where I am – but I refuse to jump at their shadow for the rest of my life. To answer your question, no, it's not safe. If you haven't worked out by now that you need to keep your eyes open and your blade sharp, then no amount of warning from me will be able to change that."

She stomped out of the cottage, unable to bear his stark expression a moment longer. Bailey waited outside by the well, her gaze fixed off in the middle distance. Tension rode in the line of her shoulders and her muscles quivered as though she'd break into a gallop at the slightest noise.

"What is it?" Devlin drew his sword from the sheath down his back and strode to the deathcharger's side. "What do you sense? Is it the Hunters?"

Bailey's nostrils dilated as she lifted her head, sampling air thick with magic. "No. Strange."

"Strange, there's an enemy but you're not sure who it is? Or strange, it's Halloween and the veil between worlds is the thinnest it will be all year?" Ivory knelt in the leaves beside the front door and closed her eyes, listening to the whispers of her ancestors.

"Everything's louder than normal, stronger, but I don't feel anything out of place."

After a long moment, Bailey shook her head.

"All Hallow's Eve is a difficult time for us," Devlin said eventually. "Everything feels ... overwhelming."

Ivory nodded. "Of course. When all the layers of magic come together in chaos, it is demonkind who feel it the strongest."

"I ... really?"

"Yes. That's why people traditionally fear those with demonic blood on Halloween; if ever we're to lose our minds, it's on a day like today." Ivory drew a deep breath, then let it out slowly. "If you can learn to control it however, it makes us infinitely more powerful – which, as far as the ritual is concerned, is a very good thing."

Pushing upright, Ivory dusted her knees, retrieved the picnic basket, and strode off towards the forest. They passed through the innermost wards a minute later, the magic shimmering the air around them. A chill pervaded the air as they walked through the second, and when they came to the final, outermost layer, Devlin stopped.

"I don't like this. Wouldn't we be better off doing the ritual inside, where you're safer?"

"The wards would interfere." Ivory waved a hand through the air, feeling the unusually strong energy slip through her fingers like molasses. "We have to find somewhere neutral – a place where all five elements meet."

"All five?"

"Earth, air, fire, water ... spirit." Ivory smiled at his stunned expression. "Why else do you think a pentagram has five points? Don't worry, I know just the place – it'll take us an hour or so to get there, but it'll be worth it."

"And what if the Hunters turn up?" Devlin waved an arm at the forest, as though he expected a horde of demon hunters to materialise the moment they left the safety of the wards. "You may not fear their shadow, but I do. I know Gawain. He never gives up, and he's dangerous – he wouldn't have been a Knight of the Round Table otherwise. To build an organisation like the Hunters proves his ability to inspire blind loyalty hasn't deteriorated over time. If they find us …"

"Then we'll deal with it." Ivory glared at him, one fist propped on her hip. "We cleansed our trails again last night after we got home; we're as safe as we can possibly be. Unless you're procrastinating for another reason?"

Devlin flinched, but after a long moment he sheathed his sword and swung onto Bailey's back with a practised movement. When he extended a hand down to Ivory, she gave him the basket and set off into the forest on foot. A long-suffering sigh echoed behind her before Bailey trotted to catch up, her giant hooves almost silent on the soft earth.

Perhaps it was silly not to ride, but Ivory couldn't bring herself to be so close to Devlin knowing that in little more than an hour she might lose him forever. Even astride Bailey, his cinnamon and sandalwood scent taunted her and she clenched her teeth against the urge to climb up behind him, bury her face in his shoulder for no other reason than to breathe him in and pretend, just for a moment, that she wasn't alone.

The terrain dipped and before long they came to a wide, well-lit gully, where one of the forest's many winding streams burbled happily out of a small cave in the side of the earth. Bailey picked her way in from the shallow end, pausing a moment to sample the stream's fresh water. Devlin dismounted to join Ivory at the mouth of the cave, eyeing the low-roofed entrance and shadowy interior with obvious doubt.

"It's bigger inside," she murmured.

He adjusted his head so that it fit better into the crook of his elbow and frowned. "It looks …"

"What?"

"Like a tomb."

Ivory took the picnic basket from him with a low laugh. "I prefer to think of it as atmospheric."

She ducked into the cave before he could answer, leaving the sunlight behind. As promised, the interior was larger than the entrance made it appear, the stream bisecting a space large enough for four people to comfortably stretch out in before narrowing to a melon-sized tunnel low in the far wall, from where the water flowed clear and cold. The bank of the stream rose sharply before flattening to soft earth that, though cool to touch, was dry enough to sit on.

Setting her basket by the entrance, Ivory flipped the lid and began to rummage for the things she needed. She was aware of Devlin speaking quietly to Bailey outside, and the deathcharger's gentle, whinnied answer – no words, just a heartbreak so huge it made Ivory's eyes itch. When Devlin ducked through the opening of the cave, Ivory didn't look up. Couldn't, else she might lose the fragile hold she had on herself and expose a level of vulnerability she'd thought long hardened.

"Hey," he said eventually, the word so modern it sounded strange from his lips.

Pick me, her heart whispered. *Please, pick me.*

Ivory cleared her throat and pointed at the dirt covered floor. "Hey. Lie down over there and we'll get started."

"Wait." Devlin fell to his knees at her side, catching her wrist so she couldn't turn away. "I wanted to say—"

"Don't," Ivory hissed, jerking from his grasp. "Don't thank me, don't wish things were different, don't say goodbye. Do. Not."

He pressed his lips together, looking unutterably sad. "I'm sorry."

"Don't do that, either," Ivory whispered, smoothing the hem of her sweater. "You don't owe me anything, least of all an apology."

Silence fell, broken only by the trickle of the stream and the sound of Ivory's breathing – which seemed wobbly and much too fast, even to her. Devlin's hand twitched and for a moment she feared what she would do if he reached for her again, but instead, he moved to lie down where she'd indicated.

Once his body was settled, Ivory took his head and placed it against the stump of his neck, creating the illusion of a whole, and sat back on her heels. "Ready? Because once I begin, you need to lie very still."

This time, when he reached out, Ivory let Devlin capture her hand and bring it to his lips, where he pressed a kiss to her knuckles. "Thank you."

Blinking back tears, Ivory nodded. She extended a clawed finger to draw sigils in the dirt, but it shook so violently the first of the runes had to be smudged out.

Pick me. Please, pick me.

"Hey." Devlin squeezed her fingers, his voice unbearably tender. "It's okay. Whatever happens, I promise I'll set your ancestor free."

Ivory blew out a breath. "I know."

Devlin's fingers slipped from hers, the loss like a physical blow – but this time, her hand was steady when she began to draw. The sigils flowed to a rhythm of their own, a long stream of demonic that formed a circle around Devlin's body. When the last of the runes connected to the first, the circle started to hum, a deep, resonant sound that vibrated through Ivory's bones and made the hairs on her arms stand on end. Guided by both instinct and magic, she pulled ingredients from her basket one by one, popping their lids off to flick pinches of this and that into the circle. For each new reagent she added, the hum changed pitch and one by one, the runes began to glow – a soft, earthy orange that became steadily brighter until it seemed impossible that nothing was on fire. Ivory lifted her thumb to her lips and bit down until blood welled, sharp and metallic on her tongue.

Pick me. Pick me. Pick me.

Ivory held her hand over the top of the circle and locked eyes with Devlin one final time. "Good luck."

Blood dripped from the tip of her thumb to land in the centre of his chest, causing the demonic circle to hiss like an over-boiling pot. Dark smoke billowed from the ground, wrapping Devlin's body until he was obscured from view – but she didn't need to see to know the moment his spirit slipped beyond the veil. She could feel it in the way her chest ached, in the way hot, fat tears spilled down her cheeks and her throat thickened with the urge to scream.

She clenched her hand into a fist and rolled to her feet, leaving the basket where it lay in her haste to exit a cave whose atmosphere had become suddenly stifling. Outside, she gulped great breaths of air, bracing herself against the sturdy wall of the gully until the world stopped spinning. Something moved by the stream and Ivory blinked her eyes until they cleared, drinking in the sight of Bailey with her head lifted to the morning sunlight, coat shining and mane fluttering in the breeze. She looked magnificent and utterly alone, and before Ivory knew what she was doing, she'd crossed the gulf between them to throw her arms around the deathcharger's neck.

"It's done," she said, though they both knew it. "Now, we wait."

"Yes."

"How are you so calm? I feel like I want to murder someone."

Bailey turned, then, lashes lifting on eyes burning with infernal green light. "Love."

"Love?" Ivory cracked a harsh laugh. "You're calm because you love him?"

The deathcharger tipped her head to the side. "Not me."

"Huh?"

"Love," Bailey whickered. "You love."

"*Me?* I'm not in love with Devlin." Ivory bopped Bailey's nose, undeterred when the deathcharger's lip pulled back to reveal a mouth full of fangs several inches long. "I've only known him a couple of days."

Bailey shrugged. "Demon."

"I don't care how different demons are; that's just ludicrous. It's not enough time."

The deathcharger's lips pursed and when she spoke, her words came out slow and measured. "Love doesn't keep time."

Ivory stared.

Love doesn't keep time.

She opened her mouth to deny Bailey again but the words wouldn't come. The deathcharger's expression softened and she nudged at Ivory with her nose until there was little option but to stroke her soft, shiny coat.

"I'm in love with him?" Ivory cleared her throat, but the squeak in her voice remained. "How can you tell?"

"Smell."

"Smell ..."

"Energy." Bailey's ears flickered. "Love smells match."

Ivory frowned. "I ... gross?"

"Love," Bailey insisted. Her brow furrowed and her voice dropped until it was almost a hiss. "Fight?"

"You want me to fight love?" Ivory blinked, realising the atmosphere had stilled as though the wildlife held their breath. "No ... you want to know if I'll fight *for* love."

"Yes." Bailey angled her head towards the forest. "Fight Hunters for love."

Ivory glared into the trees, as though she could see through to the menace beyond. "How many Hunters, Bailey?"

"Many."

"Damn." Ivory let out a long breath, glancing back at the cave where Devlin lay inert. "He might not come back, you know. My ancestor might not set him free."

Bailey shrugged. "Maybe."

Maybe. Maybe. Maybe.

Ivory growled deep in her chest. "You're asking me to risk my life on a chance! The tiniest, slimmest, most ridiculous chance."

This time, Bailey chuckled. "Yes."

Shadows began to form beyond the treeline. The energy of Halloween swirled around her, filling her with the chaos of mingling worlds. It would be easy to corral the energy – she could use it to escape, to disappear without a trace and return to her old life, forgetting that she'd ever met an ex-knight named Devlin whose head wasn't attached to his shoulders. She could abandon him the way the entire world had abandoned her, and once the Hunters were done, there'd be nobody left alive to say that she'd been wrong. Sure, reality would become a more terrible place than it was already ... but Ivory would live.

Alone.

For the rest of her life.

Love doesn't keep time.

"Ah, shit. I'm in love with Devlin," Ivory whispered.

Bailey's tail flicked. "Yes."

The moment hung, refracting in the morning light with the brilliance of a diamond. Ivory wanted to capture the painful beauty of it even as she longed to banish the vulnerability it created – but the moment persisted until she had little choice but to accept the inevitable. She loved Devlin, and if she wanted the chance to see him again, she and Bailey had to buy whatever time he needed to make peace with his sins.

"All right." Ivory lifted her chin, allowing the energy of All Hallow's Eve to wash through her body, forming it as nature had intended from the beginning. "Time to show Gawain what a real demon is made of."

A FORK IN THE ROAD

DEVLIN WASN'T SURE WHAT he'd expected to find beyond the veil, but a cute little cottage in a street paved with well-swept cobblestones wasn't it. One moment, he'd closed his eyes against the billowing rush of smoke that filled Ivory's demonic circle and the next, he opened them to find himself standing, head in hand, beside a white picket fence complete with an ornamental gate and a novelty mailbox in the shape of a birdhouse.

"Well," he said, looking down at the not at all ornamental bird sitting on top of the mailbox. "What now?"

The bird, small enough to fit in the palm of his hand, fluffed up unnaturally blue feathers and cheeped at him. When Devlin didn't immediately respond, it hopped to the edge of the mailbox roof, pecked his nose and flew away.

"Ow," Devlin muttered, shifting his grip so he could rub the tiny ache. He glanced up and down the street, but the collection of eclectic abodes lay silent. The road was so clean it sparkled in the bright sunlight and the scent of flowers hung pleasantly in the air, as though someone had taken a snapshot of the perfect spring morning and imprinted it on the environment for all eternity.

Devlin turned his attention to the cottage in front of him; small, with a vibrant green lawn and bright flowers smiling from equally bright window boxes. The windows were round, the walls rendered in bright violet, the shutters and trim a brilliant white. The route from gate to covered porch was marked by quaint grey stepping stones placed just far enough apart to traverse comfortably and the front door, hung with a wreath of twisted branches, swung open as Devlin watched.

The woman in the doorway was unremarkable with her short brown hair, dark eyes and smattering of freckles – but he'd recognise her anywhere, at any time, for she was indelibly marked upon his stained soul as the woman who'd cursed him as he stole her life with callous hands. They stared at each other for long minutes, and then, to Devlin's utter astonishment, her features crinkled into a welcoming smile.

"Are you going to stand there all day?" she asked, waving a hand in his general direction. "Or are you going to come inside?"

"Uh," Devlin replied.

The woman laughed, stepping back from the doorway. "Come along now, Sir Devlin. My tea's getting cold."

With little other option, Devlin traversed the gently meandering pathway and alighted on the porch. It creaked under his weight and he flinched, wishing abruptly for his sword – which promptly appeared on his back, in the leather scabbard he'd worn for thousands of years.

"You won't need that," his host said cheerfully. "Leave it in the umbrella stand."

"Apologies," Devlin murmured as he stepped across the threshold. "I don't know where it came from."

"It's part of you," she answered, reaching around him to close the door with a click. "You thought you needed it, and so it appeared. In my experience, men tend to be irrationally attached to their swords – but no harm will come to you in this place, I promise." She paused, looking down at his face from eyes so dark a brown they were almost black, and smiled. "My name is Jenniker, but you can call me Jenn."

Jenn. He'd murdered a woman named Jenn, with brown hair, freckles, and a sweet face that held definite traces of Ivory in it. Devlin swallowed heavily. "I never knew your name."

"No," she said breezily, tugging him into a well-lit lounge with curved walls, a hand-woven rug and several brightly upholstered arm chairs. "It wasn't really necessary in your line of work."

"I'm sorry."

Jenn snorted. "Little late for that now, isn't it? Sit down while I fetch my tea."

Devlin watched her bustle away in her blue homespun dress and then, for lack of anything better to do, perched on the edge of an armchair and balanced his head on his knees. When Jenn returned, she had a cup of tea in one hand and a plate of biscuits in the other. Her smile was still firmly in place as she sat, took up a biscuit and bit into it, watching Devlin as she chewed.

"So," she said, swallowing noisily. "Why are you here?"

"I beg your pardon?"

"Here, in this cottage." Jenn waved her biscuit in emphasis. "Sitting on my chair as though it might swallow you whole at any second?"

"I came to repent." Devlin straightened his spine and looked deep into her eyes. "I took something precious from you and your family. I came to beg forgiveness, and to help sever the ties which have bound us together all these years."

"Hmm." Jenn laid a hand over her ribs, in the exact place Devlin's blade – the blade currently in her umbrella stand – had slid home. She chewed her lower lip a long moment, dark eyes solemn as she looked him up and down in exactly the way Ivory had done when they'd first met. "Are you sure?"

Devlin's jaw dropped. "What? Of course I'm sure."

"Well, then, I suppose I have some things that need to be said." Jenn ate the rest of her biscuit and then picked up another.

"I hated you when I first arrived here. I didn't get to see my children grow up, or walk into the twilight at my husband's side. The wound you caused when you drove your sword through my heart never healed, and I have lingered in pain ever since." She dusted biscuit crumbs from her dress, then leaned forward and braced both elbows on her knees. "I transferred my powers to you in anger. I wanted you to know what it was like to become the thing you hunted; to understand the terror demons face when we're persecuted simply for existing – as though we are lesser simply by virtue of the fact that we are different." Her lips twisted. "I will not argue that evil demons do not exist, but nor will you argue, I think, that there is not evil in all beings, no matter their species. Evil is not a birthright; it's a choice, and every individual has an opportunity to make it."

The words hit hard, and Devlin closed his eyes to absorb each blow. Manners dictated he speak, the words ragged as they tore from his deepest self. "I wish I'd made a better choice."

Jenn sipped her tea, lashes lowered.

"Here's the thing, though," she said at last. Setting the cup down, she moved from her chair to kneel at Devlin's feet. "You suffered, too. Tied together as we are, every time I close my eyes, I see through yours. I have witnessed your solitude, your life with Bailey and recently, your search for a way to pay your debt." With gentle fingers, Jenn flipped a lock of Devlin's hair back from his face. "Your attitude change, the way you interact with Ivory, the magnetic pull of your attraction ... You have become more than the sum of your parts, Sir Devlin, and though you came here to restore your honour, I will tell you that you never truly gave it up – you learned your lesson in humility and have grown from it."

"But your husband," Devlin murmured. "Your daughters."

"When they died, they passed through here," Jenn smiled. "They were allowed to visit with me for a while, and once you and I are no longer tethered, I'll be free to join them on the other side. We will be together again."

"That's why I'm here," Devlin choked, daring to grasp her hand with his larger one. "I promised Ivory I would set you free, and I will, no matter what you demand of me."

"Is that what Ivory wants?"

"What?" Devlin blinked. "What do you mean?"

Jenn pursed her lips. "Ivory's been kicked more times than any one creature should have to endure. If I take your soul as payment then she'll gain the power to assume a human form and live a human life, but she'll face that life alone. And that, I think, would be *my* crime." She paused. "Unless you don't want to stay with her?"

"Of course I want to stay with her," Devlin snapped. "She's beautiful and funny and wicked and real. I want her to be happy more than I want my next breath."

"And yet you're willing to give away that next breath."

"If that's what you need to be free, then yes." Devlin swallowed. "I don't *want* to leave her, though; or Bailey. And I don't really know how to be a demon—"

"That's because you've been stuck halfway all this time." Jenn crossed both arms over her chest. "Or are your old prejudices still a problem?"

"No," Devlin growled. "There's nothing wrong with being a demon; I know that now."

"Good." Jenn chewed her lower lip. "Do you love her?"

Devlin froze. "Love?"

"You heard me. Yes or no?"

"Um." Heat crept over his cheeks, and he looked away from her piercing gaze. "I have no idea if Ivory feels—"

"*Yes or no?*"

"Yes!" he cried, slapping a hand against his thigh. "Yes, I love her – but I cannot, in all good conscience, devote myself to her knowing that my continued existence keeps you tethered to this plane. When I first sought Ivory, I knew only that she was the path to this moment, where I could get down on my knees and beg for absolution. In a short space of time, she became everything – but no matter how much my heart belongs to Ivory, you have a prior claim upon my life. If you demand it, I will give it to you."

"Even if it means leaving Ivory alone? And Bailey, who has followed you so long and loved you so well?"

Devlin let his lashes drift shut, forcing words through the agony in his chest. "Even then."

"Then here is your penance, Sir Devlin." Jenn cleared her throat. "To repay the debt you owe, you will return to the living realm as a demon and dedicate your days to making a better world. You will take your second chance in both hands and you will squeeze every drop of laughter, joy, sadness, fury, passion and *life* out of it, filling your days with such substance that they overflow." She took a step forward, jaw set. "Most of all, you will do that which is a knight's highest sworn duty: you will protect. You will fight for those who cannot fight for themselves. You will stand for the people who do not quite fit; the people who are hunted and beaten and excommunicated for no other reason than that they are different. You will be an avatar for the alternative, and you will demonstrate to the non-believers that honour is a choice that can be made every single day." Jenn jabbed a finger into Devlin's bicep. "You will start your life over again and this time, you'll do it right. *That* is the price I demand of you."

Devlin stared, his stomach flipping with such speed he wondered if it might rebel, despite having had nothing inside it for millenia. "And Ivory?"

"Earn her." Jenn caught hold of Devlin's hair, lifting his face closer to her own. "Teach her happiness and love. Though the mists of time separate us, she is still family, my many-times granddaughter. If you truly cherish her, Sir Devlin, then you may spend the rest of your life proving your worth – and I will forgive you for what you stole."

Tears welled in Devlin's eyes and he made no effort to blink them back. "Thank you."

"Is that a yes?" A soft hand landed on his shoulder. "Please say yes, Devlin. Let this end in peace."

"Yes," Devlin croaked, shaking all over. "I accept the terms of your penance."

"About time," drawled a new voice.

With gentle fingers, Jenn wiped the tears from Devlin's eyes and set his head into his lap. When she leaned away, it was to reveal a man slouched against the far wall, hands stuffed casually into the pockets of his long, black coat. Tall and slender, with an angular face and thick hair the colour of eggplant that stuck out at all manner of angles, he looked young and unassuming – but the energy which crackled off him sent chills over Devlin's skin.

"Who are you?" Devlin asked, climbing slowly to his feet.

"Myself." The man shrugged, his voice both smooth and raspy at the same time, as though he'd drunk warm honey to soothe a sore throat but it hadn't yet taken complete effect. "I suppose you might say that I am ..." his lips twisted into a grin, bringing an unholy light to eyes a darker shade of aubergine than his hair. "I am the Guardian of this place."

Jenn rolled her eyes. "He doesn't understand that joke."

"It wasn't for him," the newcomer said, still grinning. Just as quickly as it had come, his amusement faded and those unusually coloured eyes locked on Devlin. "I'm here to set Jenn free, and send you back where you belong."

"You're ..." Devlin fought the urge to take a step back. "A reaper?"

The man tilted his head to the side, brow furrowed and lips moving as though talking to himself. "No," he said at last. "Not *a* reaper."

Unease trickled through Devlin's veins as he glanced at Jenn, but she only looked annoyed. "Can we get on with this, already? Some of us are in pain, you know."

"Of course." Pushing off the wall, the man removed long, thin hands from his pockets and beckoned with the elegance of a dancer. His black coat billowed over a fitted black t-shirt and tattered black jeans, hinting at a frame that was unnaturally thin – yet when he wrapped his fingers around Devlin's wrist, his grip was like steel. "You'll need this."

Devlin stared down at the crimson sword that had been, up until that very moment, in the umbrella stand. "I will?"

"Oh, yes." Those aubergine eyes unfocussed, the man's papery voice taking on an eerie, singsong cadence. "There's a man who, despite all the evidence placed before him, clings to his own hatred. He rides a wave of destruction as though it were justice and wears a cloak woven from twisted dogma."

"Gawain." Devlin hissed out a breath. "I knew something was out of place when we left the wards." He took his sword, and the man blinked as though surprised to find himself amongst company. "I appreciate the warning."

Another blink, and slowly, the man's face resumed some semblance of animation. "Is that what that was?"

"Yes," Jenn replied, reaching out to prise the man's fingers from Devlin's wrist. They came one at a time, as though breaking the rictus took concerted effort – but then the man shook his hand with the same liquid elegance as before, and the moment was lost. Jenn prodded him gently in the chest. "Come on, now. The sooner the better for everyone, I think."

"Yes, you're right." The man positioned Jenn and Devlin so that they stood facing one another, and waved his long fingers between them. "Head. Heart."

Devlin raised a brow but Jenn seemed to understand, for she took his head and placed it upon the stump of his neck, smoothing her palms over the place where skin and bone had been severed. She lifted her eyes to Devlin's and took a deep breath. "Take care of her."

"I will." After a moment's hesitation, Devlin gingerly laid his hand over her heart – where, so many long years ago, he had driven his sword. "Thank you."

Jenn smiled and the strange man stepped in close, gripping one of their shoulders in each of his hands, long lashes dragging his eyes shut. "You're welcome," he said. "May you both find peace beyond the weave."

Devlin frowned but before he had a chance to consider the odd phrase, scalding heat washed through his body and everything went black.

YOU'RE NOT EVIL, I'M EVIL

IVORY HELD HER PLACE at Bailey's side as the trees rustled, her sharper eyesight picking out more than twenty silhouettes lurking among the trunks.

"You have the high ground and the advantage of numbers, Gawain," she called. "And still you choose to hide like a coward."

A sussurus of whispers licked through the air as Gawain Braybrook stepped out of the trees. He'd muddied his blond hair and pale skin, his clothes a mixture of the browns and greens which comprised the forest – but nothing could disguise the hard light of loathing in blue eyes so bright they almost glowed.

"I didn't want you to flee like the animal you are," he boomed, fisting both hands on his hips. "Do not fear, unholy creatures. We're here to grant you the mercy of the light."

Ivory raised an eyebrow as Gawain lifted his face to the sun, showing off the strong column of his dirt-smudged throat. "Ego, much?"

Bailey snorted, her great shoulders shaking with mirth.

"Do you know what you have walked into, Master Hunter?" Ivory brandished her elongated claws. She'd had to forgo her liniments in order to properly cast Devlin's circle but in her true form, that was of little matter. "Do you understand what Halloween is?"

Gawain's eyes blinked open. "Halloween is the one day of the year where the veil between worlds is thinnest, and demonic power rises to new heights. I've fought – and killed – enough of your kind to know that not even a day like today can save you."

A chorus of clicks echoed through the clearing and Ivory chuckled, locking each of the locations into the vast stillness at the centre of her mind. "I suppose we'll see, won't we?"

Ivory took two running steps forward and launched herself at Gawain amidst a chorus of firing crossbows. His lips spread in a victorious smile as the projectiles whizzed through the air – and then Ivory was gone, reappearing behind the first of the Hunters who'd been stupid enough to cock his weapon where she could hear it. He hadn't even registered her presence before she wrapped her clawed hands around his head and jerked, breaking his spine with an audible snap. His crossbow tumbled to the ground and Ivory scooped it up, stepping through space to the second location in her mind. This time, she appeared in front of her wide-eyed opponent – a woman whose astonishment remained even as Ivory put a crossbow bolt right between her eyes. Rather than bother to reload, Ivory snapped the crossbow in two and discarded the pieces, collecting the next one.

"Where is she?" Gawain roared. "Find her!"

Ivory's lips quirked as she made the short teleport to the third archer on her mental map. He went down as silently as his companions. As she destroyed the old crossbow and exchanged it for a fresh one, she caught a hint of elderoot and arkhberry on his clothing.

"Carrying poison, little Hunter?" Ivory leaned over the body, following her nose to the small vial tucked in his top pocket. "Tsk, tsk."

Ivory popped the lid and swallowed the contents. The raspy elderoot tingled through her veins, dragging with it the slower, if more deadly, syrupy arkhberry. She shivered as the energy whispered against her own, flowing down to turn the tips of her fingers a deep plum colour. When she flexed her hands, poison dripped from the end of her claws. She smiled.

A ringing neigh broke through the cacophony of combat and Ivory turned to see Bailey standing on her hind legs, hooves flashing in the sunlight as she fought off two Hunters who stabbed at her with long, wicked knives. The deathcharger dipped and struck, the crack of bone loud as she landed a blow – and then she screamed as a crossbow bolt sank deep into her hindquarters.

"No," Ivory whispered. "I don't think so."

She teleported out to the sound of Bailey's rage. The Hunter who'd shot already had his bow lifted and loaded, and Ivory shunted the muzzle of the weapon aside as she raked her poisoned claws across his face. He dropped to the ground screaming, body convulsing, eyes rolling back in his head.

In the gully, Bailey's opponents pushed in close, seeking to take advantage of her wounds. She let out a shrieking roar as she slashed open the chest of one Hunter and tore out the throat of another – but one hind leg dragged on the ground, the wound in her haunches oozing black blood.

"I'm coming," Ivory whispered, focussing on the final spot marked on her mental map. "Hold on, Bailey."

She teleported again.

The last Hunter was prepared, pulling the trigger on her bow as soon as Ivory appeared. The bolt bit into her side and she hissed as she grabbed at the weapon, yanking it out of the woman's hands and then clobbering her with it. The Hunter's skull crushed with a pulpy sound, and that was that.

Perhaps a better person would have been more remorseful – but as Ivory teleported to Bailey's side, kicking away a short sword that glowed with enchantments, she was glad she lacked a conscience. If this was evil, this great pounding drum in her chest that demanded she *fight*, then she'd embrace it.

"I'm here," she gasped, pulling the crossbow bolt from her

side and driving it into the throat of a Hunter with a machete. "I'm here, Bailey."

"Me," Bailey huffed, pivoting so that Ivory could pull the bolt from her hindquarters. She grunted, nostrils flaring, and then ducked the whistling swing of an axe. Ivory stepped beneath the guard of the man who'd swung it and jammed the crossbow bolt up under his ribs. He groaned as he fell, axe clattering to the ground at her feet.

"What does this buy you?" Ivory called, scooping the weapon up in both hands. She glared up at where Gawain lounged against the side of the gully. "Watching your people die? What's the point?"

The Master Hunter tipped his head to one side as the remaining Hunters closed in. "There's honour in dying for your cause. I stand witness to their sacrifice."

"Sacrifice?" Ivory spat on one of the corpses. Her saliva hissed, and the scent of burning flesh filled the air. "This isn't sacrifice, Gawain. This is a slaughter. Honour is nothing but an illusion, and you might be the greatest charlatan I've ever met."

"I am no more and no less than what you see before you." Gawain's smile faded as he took a step forward. "I am the Master of Hunters, and you're nothing but a beast."

Ivory raised an eyebrow. "You think you're so great, why don't you come down here and prove it?"

"No," Bailey huffed, shaking her head. "Bad."

"I don't care. I'm sick and tired of this pompous asshole." Flipping the axe in her hands, Ivory flung it in Gawain's direction.

The Master Hunter caught the weapon with a slapping sound that echoed through the clearing. He dropped the axe to the ground, uncurling his fingers to reveal a bloodied stripe across one palm. "Do you know what I am, demon?"

"Clumsy?" Ivory suggested, wiping the back of her mouth with one wrist. "Conceited? Crazy? Oh!" She snapped her fingers. "I know. How about a royal cu—"

"A healer," Gawain cut in. He wiggled his fingers and the cut on his palm began to glow with soft golden light. When it faded, his skin was smooth and whole. "All true Braybrooks are."

"Are you planning to heal the demon out of me?" Ivory spat on the ground at her feet. The earth sizzled. "I'm terrified."

"It means," Gawain continued as though she'd never spoken, "that I know an awful lot of ways to ensure you don't die. Painful ways."

"Seems counterproductive, since you've been trying to kill us this whole time."

"Have I?" Gawain smiled then, broad and icy. "You'll die, never fear – it'll just be on my terms. You see, unlike other Braybrooks, I have a rather nifty little trick up my sleeve. Want to know what it is?"

"You're going to tell me anyway," Ivory muttered. "That's how this works."

"Indeed. Here's the secret, then – the last one you'll ever hear." Gawain lowered his voice to conspirational whisper. "I can heal from a distance."

The Master Hunter clenched his fist and agony shot through Ivory's bones, arching her back and drawing a scream from her lips. Every injury she'd sustained during the battle flared to life, burning as though someone had poured hot acid onto her flesh. Beside her, Bailey groaned and dropped to her knees, eyes squeezing shut.

"Shit," Ivory gasped. The same golden glow that had emanated from Gawain's hand began to shine through her skin, burning with the fire of a thousand suns.

"Shit," Bailey agreed, shuddering as golden light spilled from her wounds. "So shit."

Gawain opened his hand and the pain subsided. Ivory's wounds were healed, but she felt as though she'd gone head-to-head with a mountain. She forced her head up, glaring from beneath heavy brows. "I'm going to kill you."

"I don't think so," Gawain chuckled. His face turned hard, eyes flicking to the left. "Again."

The nearest Hunter stepped forward and Ivory couldn't even begin to lift her limbs as he rammed his sword deep into her gut. She groaned, vision swimming.

"Will you die this time?" Gawain wondered, tapping his chin in thought. "I wonder."

The Hunter pulled his sword out and Ivory flopped onto her belly as the horrible, healing agony tore through her system. It was like reliving the original wound all over again, along with the burning aches and itches one normally associated with recovery – except instead of over several days or weeks, she endured it in moments, with the wattage dialled up to maximum. When the pain passed, she lay panting in the dirt, bile scratching at the back of her throat.

"No," Gawain chuckled. "No, I don't think you'll die this time – but the next? Or the one after that? Who knows?"

Laughter bubbled up in Ivory's chest. She giggled as the Hunter drove his sword through her spine, and then presumably into Bailey, judging by the way the deathcharger screamed. When the hideous burn of Gawain's magic swept through her once more, her giggles evolved into cackles, tears streaming down her cheeks. She laughed as the magic faded, pressing her face hard against the earth. It whispered to her in demonic, a soft, barely there sound that grew and grew until the ground began to rumble, the trees creaking and rustling as they swayed in time to an ancient song.

"What's that?" Gawain demanded, bracing one arm against the earthen wall of the gully. "What's happening?"

Ivory flipped onto her back, laughter echoing in the air as she caught hold of the Hunter who'd tortured her and severed the tendons in his ankle. He crumpled with a shriek, poison surging through his veins, and Ivory grabbed onto the sword he'd conveniently driven into the ground and hauled herself to her feet.

"That? It's what I was waiting for." Ivory snorted another

laugh, looping an arm around Bailey's neck as the deathcharger struggled upright at her side. "This is where it really begins, Gawain. Listen to the wind, to the earth, to the trees. Can you hear it? Can you feel it?"

"What?" Gawain growled, eyes darting all around. "*What?*"

Ivory grinned. "Your old friend Sir Devlin is awake."

THE DEMON WITHIN

ENERGY BUBBLED AND SEETHED and within it, Devlin's blood. Heat like he'd never known surged through his soul, melting down what had once been a man and forging something new in its place. It was overwhelming in such a way that he couldn't think, couldn't flinch, couldn't do anything other than endure, clinging to the threads of his sanity until even that was swept away by an endless vortex of sensation.

Through the mist and fire and howling wind came a sound; soft and stuttering at first, then gaining in intensity until the furious thumping drowned out everything around it, filling Devlin's mind with the steady, pulsing thunder of a bass drum. It wasn't until his eyes flew open and his lungs drew a sharp, painful breath that he realised the incessant sound was his heart, beating for the first time in thousands upon thousands of years.

And if his heart beat ...

The atmosphere was full of thick, grey smoke, but Devlin didn't need to see to lift his hands to his throat. To start at the base with trembling fingers and feel slowly upwards, along the column of his neck, over the thin ridge of scarring, to his head.

His head, which was attached to his neck.

His head, attached to *his* neck, on a body that was very much *alive*.

Emotion swept through Devlin in a tide, and for a moment he lingered on the precipice of both laughter and tears. He spent several long, distracted moments simply breathing, hands moving up and down his neck to be sure the moment was real. When he felt brave enough, Devlin turned his head to one side and then the other, glorying in the simple bunch and release of muscles that hadn't been connected for millenia.

The smoke began to thin and Devlin sat up, grinning as his head came along for the ride. He hunched his shoulders, leaning forward to brace against his knees; his head behaved as if it had always been attached, his neck arching and his chin tucking down against his chest.

He'd never have to pick his head up off the floor again.

Never have to tuck it under his arm, or set it down nearby in order to perform a two-handed task.

Most of all, he'd be able to kiss Ivory the way she deserved.

... a man who, despite all the evidence placed before him, clings to his own hatred. He rides a wave of destruction as though it were justice and wears a cloak woven from twisted dogma ...

Devlin blinked as the words came rushing back, euphoria turning to dread. Rolling to his knees, he waved away the last of the smoke to see the cave where Ivory had pushed him beyond the veil. He was alone, demonic runes still glowing in the dirt while Ivory's reagents littered the area around the picnic basket.

"Ivory?" He pushed to his knees and froze, arrested by the sight of long fingers that ended in wicked looking claws. Lifting first one hand and then the other, Devlin stared. He had the same skin tone as always, along with the tiny scars from his many years using a sword – but his skeletal structure was slightly different, the bones longer, the claws vicious and sharp.

He flexed his fingers in astonishment, then opened his mouth to discover his teeth were no longer blunt, human teeth but pointed like a proper predator's. Swallowing heavily, Devlin lifted his hands to his head. There, sweeping back from his temples in a deadly curl ... horns.

He had *horns*.

Heart thumping madly, Devlin looked down to discover his t-shirt in shreds. He tore off the remains of the shirt, taking in hard packed muscle that, whilst familiar, was wrapped tighter to his bones somehow, giving him a sturdier presence than he'd had before and emphasising the line of his abdominals as they tracked down to the waistband of his jeans – which clung to his buttocks and thighs as though they'd been painted on.

Demon.

He was a demon.

He'd known it was going to happen, of course, but now it was *real*, and for a wrenching moment the idea of a head on his shoulders, air in his lungs and horns on his head was too much. Then he remembered Ivory, and Jenn, and the promises he'd made, and everything settled into place with an almost audible snap.

Devlin crawled to the edge of the circle and there was a soft popping sound as the glowing characters winked out. All at once the cave filled with sound; screaming and groaning and the unmistakable thump of bodies hitting the dirt.

A growl vibrated in Devlin's throat and he pushed to his feet, swaying a moment as he rediscovered his centre of balance. He clenched his fist, wishing he had his sword – and it was suddenly there, materialising the same way it had done in Jenn's hallway. The crimson blade began to glow, steadily increasing in brightness until scarlet fire licked down the sharpened edge.

Whole. Demon. Whole. Demon. *Whole.*

The words pounded in his blood but it wasn't shame he felt, only fierce elation. This, here, was where he was meant to be. It was *what* he was meant to be.

He ducked through the cave's entrance to find the gully transformed from idyllic picnic spot to grisly nightmare. Dead Hunters littered the ground like macabre river stones and beyond, Bailey spun and ducked and twisted as she battled those who remained standing, her greater bulk preventing them from slipping down the sides of the gully to reach the entrance of the cave.

Devlin strode forward, a growl building deep in his chest as he reached Bailey's side. His sword flashed in a wide arc and two Hunters lost limbs to the blade; a third caught fire as the scarlet flames licked over the sleeve of her jacket.

"You're here," Bailey whickered, arching her neck. Pivoting in place, she delivered a swift kick to her closest opponent, knocking him back into his comrades.

"I'm here." Devlin bumped his shoulder against hers. "Where's Ivory?"

Bailey tossed her head, mane flying. "Gawain."

Devlin inspected their remaining enemies, no more than fifteen in total, then raised his gaze to the treeline at the far end of the gully. He couldn't see or hear anything beyond what was happening in front of him, but instinct said Ivory was in that direction – battling a fae knight who had thousands of years more experience than she did.

"I'll give you one chance to lay down your arms and surrender," Devlin called, directing his attention back to the Hunters in front of him. "Go, now, and live to fight another day."

Several of the Hunters faltered, but one raised her chin. "Demonic filth! So long as righteousness guides us, we will never be vanquished by one such as you!"

Devlin snorted. How similar the words were to the dogma he'd once inhaled – dogma which had led him to slaughter demons without first stopping to check if they were deserving of such a fate.

"So be it," he said, lifting his sword. The flames which licked along the blade began to intensify, crawling up Devlin's arm and leaving a scrolling crimson design in their wake.

Driven by an energy he didn't understand, Devlin twisted his sword in a preparatory movement he'd learned as a boy. The fire which had gathered up his arm surged down the blade and outward, passing through the assembled Hunters in a single, thin arc of flame. Astonishment twisted the features of every single opponent – until their bodies began to drop, cleft in half by the sizzling wave of demonic magic.

"Uh ..." Devlin stared down at his sword, where the flames had reduced until they licked along the bladed edge once more. The swirling crimson design remained etched into his skin, covering his entire arm, spreading over his shoulder and chest. "Oops."

Bailey snorted a laugh and bumped him with her shoulder. "Come."

Devlin mounted in a daze, curling the fingers of one hand through her mane as she plunged up the gully. Barely had they reached the trees when the unmistakable retort of a gun split the air, quickly followed by a second and then a third.

Bailey tore through the forest as fast as she could go, forcing Devlin to lean over her neck or risk losing his seat. They erupted into a small clearing, her hooves skidding on the forest floor as she drew up short in front of Gawain. He held a bulky looking pistol, eyes narrowed as he sighted Devlin down the barrel.

"I don't know what you thought to gain by running into the forest, little demon." The Master Hunter's voice was calm as he cocked the weapon. "If I can't kill you, I'll kill these abominations instead."

"If you don't know a distraction when you see it, you're dumber than I thought." Ivory materialised at Gawain's side, blocking his arm even as she delivered a ringing blow to the side of his head. Just as quickly as she'd appeared she was gone, winking out of existence with a speed that had Devlin's jaw on his chest. She could *teleport?*

Gawain cursed, aiming the weapon in Devlin's direction a second time. Ivory blinked back into existence less than an inch from the Hunter's face, placing her body directly in the line of fire. The gun went off and she grunted as she thrust her elbow into Gawain's throat, ripping the weapon from his hands. Devlin leapt off Bailey's back, intending to catch Ivory as she fell – but she swept Gawain's feet from under him and dropped to one knee on the Hunter's chest, the gun pointed at his head and her finger curved over the trigger.

"Call her off!" Gawain cried, eyes wide with horror. "Call her off!"

Blood covered Ivory's skin and clothes, oozing from the gunshot wounds in her ribs. Black dreadlocks hung wild about her face, lips pulled back from pointed teeth, ebony eyes glittering. The horns which curled from her head were larger than Devlin had ever seen them and judging by the gore coating the tips, Ivory knew full well how to put them to use. Her clothes, slicked to her body, highlighted the way her vertebrae were too prominent, the lines of her skeleton sleek and fluid.

She was anything but human, and she was the most beautiful thing Devlin had ever seen.

"Ivory," he murmured, lowering his sword to his side. "Are you all right?"

"I shot her," Gawain shouted. "Twice! With salt bullets! Why isn't she dead?"

"Because I'm not like most demons," Ivory purred, her voice low and deadly. She shifted her grip on the gun, laughter belling from her throat when Gawain flinched. "More interestingly, why haven't you tried your little pain-by-healing trick? Could it be that your powers don't work around salt? Why would that be, I wonder?"

"Shut up," Gawain hissed, his skin turning pale. "*Shut up.*"

Ivory turned her head ever so slightly and though her eyes never left Gawain, her voice softened. "She set you free."

"Yes," Devlin answered. "She did."

"How do you feel?"

"I feel ..." Something took flight in his chest. "I feel like I'm in love with you."

Ivory choked. "*That's* how you decide to tell me? While we're standing over an asshole?"

"Uh." Heat crept into Devlin's cheeks. "It just sort of came out."

She laughed, the sound edged in sin. "Tell me again once I've shot your ex-friend in the head."

"Wait." Devlin held up a hand and, to his surprise, Ivory's finger froze on the trigger. He took a step forward and crouched, remaining just out of Gawain's reach. "Why doesn't your magic work around salt?"

Gawain spat on the ground at his feet. "As if I'd answer that."

"Salt is demonsbane – in most cases, anyway." Ivory tilted her head in consideration. "Are you part demon?"

"Never!" Gawain bared his teeth as though their blunt, human appearance were somehow proof.

"Sounds like too strong a protest to me." Shifting the gun to one hand, Ivory wiped her fingers across a bloodied gash by Gawain's elbow. "Why don't we find out?"

"Stop that," Gawain hissed, jerking his arm away. "I'll kill you; I swear it."

"Uh huh." Ivory lifted her bloodied fingers and sniffed. "Odd."

"What?" Devlin asked.

"It's ..." she frowned, licking the pad of one finger. "He's not a demon, but ..."

"But?"

Ivory licked again, and blinked. Comprehension dawned on her face and she stared down at Gawain with a mixture of pity and amusement. "You were possessed at some point in your life. The demon's essence lingers in your system, tainting your blood – it's why salt negates your magic." She clicked her tongue against the roof of her mouth. "You know ... if the demon who possesses you ever returns, you won't be able to stop it taking you over like a puppet."

"It cannot return," Gawain hissed. "I killed it, just like I swore to kill every other demon I ever came across."

"You do realise that not every demon is capable of possession? That's a rare skill belonging to an equally rare creature." Ivory shrugged. "Whatever that demon made you do probably sucked, but genocide isn't the answer – nor will it erase the touch of a demon from your system."

"You know nothing." Gawain's hiss became a growl, and he lifted his head to press it against the muzzle of the gun. "If you're going to shoot me, then do it now – unless you're a coward?"

"No." Devlin laid one of his fingers over Ivory's wrist. "That isn't the answer."

"Why not? He'd have killed you while you lay helpless in that cave," Ivory whispered, her eyes narrowed.

"I'm not like him," Devlin retorted. "To kill someone in battle is one thing. To murder them in cold blood is another entirely."

"You think to act with honour?" Gawain barked a sharp, incredulous laugh. "You forsook everything I ever taught you. You betrayed a friendship I treasured and turned willingly into the very creature you swore to exterminate."

"That's true," Devlin agreed. "But I still owe you a debt. One of mercy, I believe."

"What?" Gawain and Ivory spluttered in unison.

"Mercy," Devlin answered. "You cut off my head with the noblest intentions, though it cost you dearly. You sacrificed your needs for mine. Now, I will do the same."

"*My* needs?" Gawain flinched back from the gun, his head thumping into the forest floor. "What could I possibly need from you?"

"Something you cannot give to yourself." With careful fingers, Devlin prised the gun from Ivory's grip. He wasn't as familiar with the weapons as many modern warriors were, but he'd picked up enough to know which end was which, and how to put it to deadly effect. "Forgiveness."

"Forgiveness?" Gawain froze for a moment, then began to thrash about, forcing Ivory to readjust her weight in order to hold him pinned. "No. You wouldn't dare."

Devlin sheathed his sword and checked the ammunition in the gun. Salt bullets, as promised. They glittered in the sun, a soft peach hue providing testament to the quality of the materials. He cocked the weapon and fired into Gawain's left shoulder.

"I forgive you for your hatred," Devlin began, raising his voice to be heard over Gawain's scream. The gun clicked a new round into the chamber, and he fired a shot into the Master Hunter's other shoulder. "I forgive you for your fear."

"I'm not afraid!" Gawain shrieked, cords bulging in his neck. "I'm not af—"

Devlin fired a round into Gawain's thigh. "I forgive you for hunting me. I forgive you for hating me. And most of all ..."

"No." Tears trickled down Gawain's face as Devlin aimed at his other leg. "Don't take this from me. You *can't*."

Devlin cocked the gun and looked his old friend in the eye. "I forgive you, Sir Gawain, once of the Round Table, for all you have done in these long, cold centuries. I, Sir Devlin, also once of the Round Table, absolve you of your sins. May you walk forever in the light."

Gawain's voice rose in an agonised wail as Devlin fired the final shot, the bullet burying deep into the flesh of Gawain's thigh. The ex-knight sobbed as he struggled against Ivory's restraining hands but the salt was already taking effect, spreading through his bloodstream and rendering the enormous warrior unconscious in a matter of moments.

"What," Ivory said, pushing away from the limp fae, "the actual fuck did I just witness?"

"An ancient knightly ritual," Devlin murmured, tossing the now-empty gun on the ground. "It is a spell of sorts, I suppose, though not in the way you'd know it. Facing your sins is painful, and takes courage, honesty and sacrifice. Four wounds, one each for those particular knightly pillars. As we heal, we remember the words that were spoken over us, and meditate to achieve peace and purity."

"You used to *shoot* each other?"

"Not specifically. The gun was an improvisation."

"Knights are stupid. Crazy and stupid." Ivory snorted and pushed to her feet. "With that much salt he'll be unconscious for a couple of days, and the wounds will take months to completely heal – if they ever do."

"Such is the price of mercy." Devlin scooped Gawain's larger body up in his arms and slung him across Bailey's back. "Will you return us to Ivory's, my friend? And then, perhaps, deposit Gawain somewhere his allies might find him when they come looking?"

Bailey inclined her head. "Yes."

"It'd be safer to kill him," Ivory pointed out. "When he's recovered, he'll hunt you again."

"Then we will meet free of debt and let fate decide the rest."

"And what of the other demons he could hurt in that time?"

"The Hunters are an organisation led by Gawain, but not personified by him." Devlin shook his head. "Regardless of whether he lives or dies, they will hunt us. Hurt us. *All of us.* But if he lives ... if he's wounded ..."

"They'll be distracted trying to help him." Ivory's lips pinched. "They might even start to wonder why he was so badly affected by salt, too. It'll buy us time to prepare that we wouldn't have had otherwise."

"Yes." Devlin pulled himself up behind Gawain, but when he extended a hand to Ivory, she frowned. "What?"

"Gawain managed to track us somehow." She motioned between them. "If we don't find the item he used, then no amount of trail cleansing will work – not long term, anyway."

"Ah. That problem, also, I can solve." Devlin reached into Gawain's shirt and drew out a heavy chain from which hung a pendant in the shape of a sword. "He didn't track us, specifically; he tracked me. With this."

Ivory eyed the necklace for a long moment. "It was yours?"

"Once, long ago. It is the sigil of a Knight of the Round Table – I gave it to Gawain before he cut off my head, both as a token of my friendship and because I felt I no longer deserved to wear it." Devlin rubbed a thumb over the pendant and sighed. "Aside from my sword, it's the only remaining memento of the life I left behind."

Ivory laid her hand over the top of Devlin's with the pendant sandwiched between them and closed her eyes. "You're a demon now and your essence has changed. This can't be used to track you any more."

"I assumed as much."

She pursed her lips. "I think you should keep it."

"Really? Why?"

"Because it's yours." Ivory undid the chain with a deft flick of her wrist, puddling it in Devlin's palm. "It deserves better than to be left with this asshole."

Devlin chuckled, slipping the pendant into the pocket of his jeans. "That's true enough, I suppose ... but it'll need a lot of cleansing before I'm ready to wear it again."

"I can cleanse it when we get home." Ivory watched him from beneath her lashes, eyes dark. "If you want."

Devlin smiled and this time, when he offered his hand, she took it. "I should like nothing more."

LOVE IS ALL WE NEED

IVORY WATCHED BAILEY DISAPPEAR into the forest and sighed. "Are you sure she'll be all right on her own?"

"Of course." Devlin paused in the act of toeing off his boots, one hand braced against the front wall of her cottage. "We killed all the Hunters and Gawain won't wake from the salt poisoning for days. Besides, Bailey can take care of herself."

Judging by the wink Bailey sent Ivory's way before she cantered off, the deathcharger wasn't worried about taking care of herself in the slightest.

"You still look worried." Warm fingers brushed her dread-locks over one shoulder, and Ivory shivered.

"I don't know what to do now," she admitted, turning her face into his open palm. The movement was instinctive and mortifying but when she made to step back, Devlin's free arm snaked around her waist.

"I do," he said, voice low and soft as he turned her to face him. "I stare deep into your eyes, just like this, and I say, 'Ivory, I love you,' and you say ..."

Ivory set her palms against Devlin's bare pectorals and let the corner of her mouth tip up. "I say, 'Devlin, you stink like dead people.'"

He laughed, the sound bright and big and beautiful. Now that his head was attached to his body, he was well over six feet and Ivory had to arch her back to meet his eyes, the infernal green colour now tinted with faint streaks of orange.

"You're a fire demon," she whispered, tracing her clawed fingers gently over one cheekbone.

"It seems that way." He shrugged. "I assumed I'd be like you, though."

"Your magic may have originated with my ancestor, but you're also a person in your own right. Your genetics will lend themselves to demonology in their own way."

"That makes sense." His gaze travelled lazily down her body, snagging on the holes in her sweater. "Do I need to dig salt bullets out of you?"

Ivory shook her head. "I've absorbed them by now."

"Really?" He lifted a brow. "I've never met a demon who could do that."

"I found mention of the talent in my family's journals, but it – like my unusual style of magic – are very rare." Ivory chewed on her lower lip a moment, weighing up best how to explain. "I'm a spirit demon. I can sense the spirits of the things around me – people, plants, the earth, and so on. In some cases, I can even manipulate them."

Devlin's eyes widened in comprehension. "The way you make liniments and potions and poultices ... you have an intrinsic understanding of which ingredients to use and your magic blends them together. That's why they're so effective."

"Yes. And in my full demon form, I can absorb elements into my body and use them to alter my genetic makeup – for example, I drank a vial of poison I found on one of the Hunters but rather than kill me, I was able to direct it to my claws." She flexed her hand in front of his face. "My ability to teleport is similar, too; I use spirits as a reference to move to that location."

"And the salt?"

"A cleanser." She smiled. "When Gawain shot me, my body absorbed the salt – it removed the poison I ingested, but that's it. I cannot use the salt, per se, but neither can it weaken or kill me."

"You should still have a hole, though." Devlin took half a step back, using his claws to shred the side of Ivory's sweater so he could inspect the bullet wound underneath. Ivory couldn't help but flinch as he brushed the back of his knuckles over her puckered flesh. "Sorry."

"You didn't hurt me. We heal fast, and I ..." she cleared her throat. "I like you touching me."

The look he gave her was full of blazing intensity. "Oh?"

Three little words hovered on the tip of Ivory's tongue, but no matter how she wished it, they wouldn't tumble out. Being alone had been difficult, but in other ways it had also been easy; nobody could abandon her if she had nobody close, after all. Now, Devlin was here, and unlike the acquaintances she'd done her best to keep at arm's length, he was inside her armour. He could tear her apart as easily as complete her, leaving her nothing but an empty shell. She couldn't go through that again. Couldn't lose again. There wasn't enough of her left to survive it.

Hysteria bubbled in her chest. Had she lost her mind? She'd wished so deeply for Devlin's love and now, here he was offering it – all she had to do was say the words.

Three. Little. Words.

Instead, she shot Devlin a coy look from beneath her lashes. "If it's all the same to you, I'd rather not trek this gore inside the house. I've a pond around the back we can scrub off in – if you're game."

Before Devlin could open his mouth to respond, she teleported the short distance to the back of the house where the pond was tucked beneath the branches of several over-arching fruit trees. Stripping down to her bra and underwear, she waded into the chest-deep water and sank beneath the surface, closing her eyes as the chill liquid slipped over her face.

Ivory hung suspended, trying to calm her racing heart. There had to be a way around this, some solution that would allow her to keep Devlin without becoming vulnerable … but dammit, he *deserved* those words, and she wanted desperately to give them to him.

The pond water lurched. Ivory's eyes flipped open as clawed fingers curled into her hair and yanked her above the surface.

"Got you," Devlin growled, lifting her until they were eye to eye. "Don't think I didn't see you trying to avoid this."

"I told you," she panted, hanging limp in his grasp. "I don't know what to do now."

"And I told you that I do." He tipped his head to one side, eyes bright with challenge. "I've never thought you a coward, Ivory, so we're going to face this head on. Are you ready?"

"No."

"Too bad, because I'm going to keep saying this until you listen. I want you. I need you. *I love you.*"

Ivory's breath caught in her throat, and she told herself the moisture on her cheeks was only pond water. She opened her mouth to deliver a scathing retort but instead, what came out was, "I love you, too."

Triumph flashed across Devlin's features and then he crushed her close, the heat of his skin a furnace as he dragged her head back and kissed her like the demon he was. Passion negated tenderness. Lips and teeth and tongues clashed in a fury of elemental need that was everything Ivory had ever wanted. She looped her arms around Devlin's neck and yanked, toppling them both backwards into the water. He didn't break the kiss as they sank, his forearms bracing them against the pebbled bottom of the pond – a pond whose water temperature rapidly changed from chill to tepid to warm as Devlin's innate fire magic responded to the desire in his blood. When the need for air became urgent, he shoved upward, hauling them both onto the soft grass at the pond's edge. Ivory let him roll her over, his eyes blazing a hot path over her soggy underwear and then back up to her face.

"I'm only going to ask once," Devlin growled, setting the tip of one claw at the top of her sternum. "After that, if I do something you don't like, it's up to you to say so."

Ivory placed her hand over his and dragged downwards, using Devlin's claw to slice through her bra so that it twanged aside in a ridiculous display of elastic enthusiasm. "You're still nicer than me," she purred. "I wouldn't have asked at all."

He lowered his head, breath teasing over her damp skin. "Yes, then?"

"Yes."

With a rumbling growl, Devlin fastened his mouth over her breast and suckled hard. The sensation went straight to Ivory's core and she gasped, arching up against the hot, hard planes of his body. While his tongue worked, Devlin shredded the remains of her bra and tossed it aside, a process he repeated with her underpants. Sharp teeth grazed her skin as he nipped his way to her other breast, nuzzling the underside before licking a path up to tease her swollen nipple with his lips.

Ivory slid her hands over his shoulders, glorying in the strength and breadth of him, the way his vertebrae were just a little too prominent – like her own. Devlin had made no attempt to assume a human appearance and the knowledge that they came together in their true forms ratcheted Ivory's need into the stratosphere. She caught at the waistband of his jeans and pulled with all her might. The denim gave way with a satisfying ripping sound and quite suddenly there was nothing between her and Devlin at all.

He groaned as he pressed against her, his erection thick and hard where it lay sandwiched between them. Ivory wriggled in a desperate attempt to get that weapon where she wanted it, but Devlin's groan turned to a chuckle and he skimmed down her body, slipping partially back into the pond as he shoved her knees up and outward.

"Devlin," Ivory made a grab for him but though she got her fingers in his hair and tugged, the damned man didn't budge an inch.

"Ivory," he purred, biting her thigh just enough for his teeth to pinch the skin. The sharp edge of pain shot through her, followed quickly by a desperate, burning heat as Devlin licked across the bite mark. "Are you in a rush?"

"Yes!"

His laughter brushed across her most sensitive flesh, and he watched her squirm over the curves and hollows of her abdomen. "Good."

The first lick of his tongue was a revelation. The next, a wicked delight. The third ... Ivory lost the ability to think of adjectives, surrendering to Devlin's caresses as she'd never surrendered to anyone or anything before in her entire life. With one hand under her lower back to lift her hips, Devlin used his other hand to tease her, his fingers gentle in contrast to the demands of his tongue and his mouth.

Ivory tried desperately to hold on but he was relentless. Her legs began to quiver and her body bucked against his face, demanding a release that only Devlin could give. She yanked at his hair and he growled against her skin, adding a level of sensation that proved too much. Her body exploded, pleasure scouring her veins, drawing a scream of ecstasy from a throat gone raw. Still Devlin gave no quarter, wringing wave after wave of pleasure from her until she thought she'd pass out – and then his mouth and hands were gone, leaving her limp and panting as he crawled up her body like a conqueror.

Knowing Devlin as she did, Ivory expected him to pause for sweet words and gentle caresses. Instead, he braced one forearm beside her head and kissed her as he thrust his cock inside her body in one long, smooth movement.

The friction was incredible. Ivory whimpered into Devlin's mouth as he drew out and snapped back in, setting her nerve endings on fire. This was no polite knight; here was a demon who knew she was his to take, just as he was hers. With every thrust, Devlin's movements grew wilder, the sounds he made desperate and raw. Ivory met him stroke for stroke, needing to stake her claim even as he branded his name on her soul.

They sought infinity in the slick glide of skin on skin, gripping so tight it was impossible to tell where one left off and the other began. They kissed and nipped and licked and gasped, words impossible while passion reigned; a furious, flickering flame that consumed Ivory until all she knew, all she was, belonged to Devlin. It was both terrifying and dizzying to look into his eyes and see the same burning emotion that dwelled in her own, to know that he wanted *her* and no-one else.

Ivory's body tightened as Devlin's movements shifted from rhythmic to desperate, a growl building in his chest as he sought to push them both ever higher. He tore his mouth from hers. Their gazes collided for a single, electric moment – then Devlin's spine locked and Ivory shattered, tumbling them over the precipice and into paradise together.

When Ivory could next think, she registered that Devlin had collapsed atop her, his face buried in her neck. His breath was hot against her skin and he rumbled in contentment, the vibration sending delicious aftershocks through Ivory's body.

"I want to do that again," he whispered, lips tickling against the skin of her throat. "And again, and again … and again."

Ivory's heart swelled and though she knew she should answer, all she could do was cling tighter, lost in the storm of emotion created by their lovemaking.

Devlin lifted his head, his lazy, sated expression sharpening as he took in her face. "What's wrong?"

"How do we … how do I …" To Ivory's horror, tears welled in her eyes and she swallowed, turning her face away.

"Hey." Devlin rolled over and sat up, arranging Ivory so that she straddled his lap. He cupped her face in both hands and kissed her softly. "I have no idea what I'm doing, either. I never expected to feel such a depth of emotion so quickly – but lack of time shouldn't make this less real, or important." Ducking his head so they were on a level, Devlin offered a wicked smile. "We'll figure out how this works."

Ivory wrapped her fingers around his wrists and let her lashes flutter shut. "It's been a long time since I've had something to lose, Devlin. If I lost you, I... I don't think I'd come back from that."

"I know." Devlin's grip tightened, his claws pricking the sides of her face. "I'm not a seer but I am – I was – a knight. Do you doubt my word?"

"You're still a knight," Ivory muttered, slumping in his grip. "Becoming a demon doesn't erase who you are; it just changes your physical makeup."

"Well, then, I'm the first Demonic Knight," Devlin announced. "And as a Demonic Knight to his Demonic Enchantress, I give you my word: whatever the future holds for us, I will not leave you. I swear it, Ivory. I am yours for as long as you wish it."

Ivory forced her eyes open, hope battling the fear that threatened to choke her. His expression was sincere, those infernal eyes brilliant.

"I'm not perfect," she said, even as she kicked herself for admitting it. "I'm morally grey at the best of times and I have a definite tendency towards bitter and jaded."

Devlin chuckled. "I know."

"And?"

"And I love you exactly as you are. Shall I list my most pressing imperfections to make you feel better?"

Ivory blushed and dropped her gaze. "No."

"I'm fairly certain Bailey has a list somewhere, should you ever care to have them officially noted." His voice was cheerful and when she looked up, it was to find him grinning like an idiot. She scowled, but that grin only widened, becoming so infectious that Ivory couldn't help but splutter a laugh. Devlin wrapped his arms around her and she set her head against his shoulder, feeling raw and vulnerable and oh-so-incredibly complete.

His embrace fell away and Ivory leaned back, brow furrowing. "What's wrong?"

"Nothing. I just had an idea." Devlin held out one hand, palm up, and then curled his fingers into a fist. Magic and heat surged around them, and he opened his fingers with a triumphant grin. "There."

In the middle of his palm, glowing red hot as though it had just come from a forge, was Devlin's pendant. The sword hung straight and true and the chain was thick and heavy – but unlike when Ivory had last seen it, tiny runes were etched down the centre of the blade. Tiny *demonic* runes which darkened as the metal cooled, and said ...

Ivory snickered. "Donut and Ivory?"

Devlin sighed. "I'm not very good at demonic, I'm afraid."

"Like this," Ivory laughed, leaning back to dip her finger in the pond and trace the correct rune on the stones beside them. "See?"

Grumbling under his breath, Devlin closed his fingers over the pendant and screwed up his face. There was a second wave of heat, less intense than the first, and when he opened his fist, the metal was once again glowing – but the runes were now correct.

Once the pendant was silver again, Devlin leaned forward and fastened the chain around Ivory's neck. The necklace was pleasantly heavy, the sword hanging point down between her breasts.

"It's Lemurian silver," she whispered, touching the intricately wrought hilt.

Devlin nodded. "We called it Fae silver back then, but it's the same thing. It was enchanted for protection once upon a time."

Ivory shifted to cover the pendant with her whole palm, brow furrowing as she listened to the soft whispers in her mind.

"It still is," she said at last, "but it's faint. I don't think Gawain was recharging it." She offered a tentative smile. "Nothing a little moonlight won't fix."

Ivory lifted her hand and together they stared down at the pendant where it hung against her chest as though it had been made to rest there. Devlin bent to kiss the hollow of her throat, his hands warm where they circled her ribs.

"Do you believe me now?" He looked up from beneath thick lashes, the afternoon sun gilding the planes of his face in gold and bringing the touches of orange in his eyes to burning life. "Do you trust me enough to see where this goes ... together?"

Biting her lip to hide how it trembled, Ivory followed the surge of emotion in her chest. "Yes. To both."

Devlin kissed her, pulling her tight against his chest as he flopped back onto the grass.

"Good," he said when they came up for air. "Because by my reckoning, we've about an hour before Bailey returns home. I say we use it wisely."

"You don't think she'd fancy the show?"

"I know she wouldn't."

"Well then, Sir Devlin," Ivory purred, kneading his chest with her claws. "You'd best put your back into it."

He did.

~ THE END ~

Thanks for reading!
Can't wait for the next instalment?
Keep up to date with all the latest shenanigans at:
www.sliceofsammy.com

ACKNOWLEDGMENTS

From the moment we decided we were doing a Halloween anthology, I knew I wanted to write about the headless horseman. Little did I realise, writing a character whose head isn't attached to his body is more than a little challenging!

The biggest thank you has to go to Mum, who on top of writing her own story was constantly on hand to workshop exactly how Devlin would be able to do things without his head, and who laughed with me every time we tried to act out how a potential situation might look with one's head held in a hand, or tucked under one arm, or balanced in the crook of an elbow, or set down on the bench.

Following on from that, I'm forever grateful to Leisl and Marnie who got behind my idea and didn't once question the insanity of it; trusting without a doubt that I'd find a way to pull this off and even laughing at my bad jokes.

Massive special mention to Bron, who did an amazing beta read and performed such duties as counting salt bullets and listening to me recount with overwhelming enthusiasm and excruciating detail how my mythological research resulted in Sir Gawain of the Round Table becoming the villain of this story. You are most awesome, I love you, thank you.

As always, thanks to my ARC team for your dedication and excitement – I am ever grateful for your efforts and hope these stories continue to make you smile for a long time to come.

To the readers; I wouldn't be half the author I am if not for you, so thank you for reading this book and I hope it brought a little spooky light into your life.

ALSO BY SAMANTHA MARSHALL

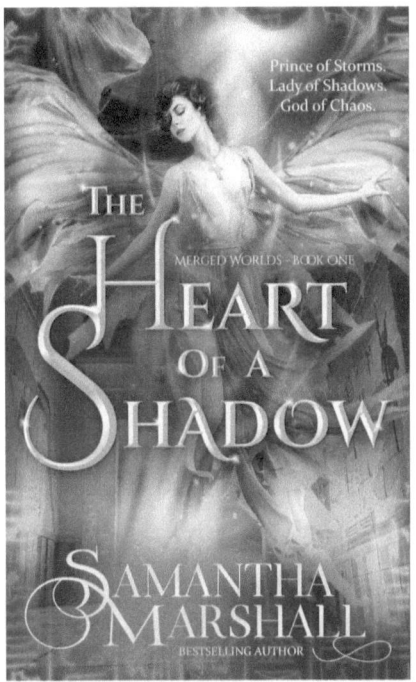

Prince of Storms. Lady of Shadows.
God of Chaos.

Bound in eternal servitude to the Atlantean royal family, dark fairy Liria Atlannon spends her days bending to the whims of her mistress. When Atlantis' youngest Princess announces her betrothal to the great Pharaoh Taos of Egypt, Liria has no choice but to follow her Princess across the sea to a kingdom - and a life - unlike anything she has known before.

As Commander of the Pharoah's honour guard, it is Prince Raiden Horushood's duty to defend his brother at all costs. He's never met a foe he couldn't conquer - until Set the Anarchist, god of war and chaos, attempts to steal the Pharoah's fiancee from her own welcome banquet. While Raiden rages helplessly in the thrall of Set's magic, Liria, the softly spoken handmaiden who spends most of her time staring at the floor, not only turns Set away but injures him in the process.

With the threat of an unpredictable god hanging overhead, Raiden begs Liria to join the Pharoah's honour guard. Though Liria aches to become part of something greater, self preservation dictates she stay away from the vital, strong, and irritatingly handsome Prince Raiden. For if the warrior angel gets too close, he'll discover that the biggest threat to Merged Egypt is not Set at all – it is Liria Atlannon, damned by the magic which shackles her soul, steals her free will and shapes her actions... until all that remains is a shadow.

Read on for a sneak preview of Chapter One!

HEARTH AND HOME

LIRIA ATLANNON LOOKED AROUND at the cool marble pillars of Princess Ione's quarters and knew she wouldn't miss it for even a moment. There was something to be said for the elegance of gold-shot marble which glowed in the light of the noonday sun, and perhaps even something to be said for the open, breezy architecture and gauzy drapes in Atlantean aqua - but for her, the paradise island of Atlantis had only ever been a prison.

Moving quietly to the edge of the balcony, Liria set delicate hands on the railing and cast her gaze out over the cheery city which glittered in the sun, shimmering marble and deep gold sandstone broken up by swathes of cloth in all the shades of the ocean. Beyond that, the azure sea lapped lazily at a pristine shore of pale sand that sparkled with hints of silver silica. A pair of Atlantean Dreadnaughts bobbed offshore, one with her steel decks unfurled like a silvered ocean lily, and the other curled in tight upon itself in preparation for an underwater journey.

"Beautiful, and yet I don't see that I will miss it."

Liria lowered her head as the Princess Ione came up beside her, lest the other woman see the way her face set into an involuntary grimace. The motion shifted her focus to her fingers, gripping tight to the balcony rail. Her skin had begun to turn the mottled blue-grey of a storm-tossed sky, her emotions slipping their leash and causing the truth of her nature to creep through. Drawing deep of the salt-laden air, Liria forced her face into smooth lines and exerted just enough power to shift her skin back to the blemish-free cream her mistress preferred.

"You won't miss it?" she asked, her voice carefully modulated to be soft and submissive. "Surely Atlantis is in your bones, your highness."

Princess Ione tossed her head. She was beautiful - exquisite, even, with long black hair that hung in perfect curls midway down her back, softly tanned skin and deep, dark blue eyes - yet there was a glitter in her gaze, an edge to her cultured smile that spoke of bitter hunger.

"No," Ione said, her lip curling. "I am meant for greater things than to be the fifth child of the ruling family of Atlantis. I am meant to be a queen."

"And so you will be," Liria answered, bowing slightly from the waist. "Your marriage to the Pharaoh of Egypt will ensure such."

An arranged marriage sounded like the worst kind of torture to Liria, but Princess Ione had been the driving force behind the entire affair. In fact, Liria's eavesdropping around the palace had her safe in the certainty that the King and Queen of Atlantis had only acquiesced to keep Ione happy; no-one had actually expected Pharaoh Taos to accept.

"Yes. Soon, I will be Queen of Egypt," Ione breathed, spreading her arms wide and tipping her head back to stare at the sky. "Soon, I will witness the technological marvel of Egypt's great airships, and view their crystal-topped pyramids with my own eyes. I shall rule over the country which stands at the forefront of science and magic, sip wine with the most powerful of gods and be bathed in the adoring praise of my subjects – while Atlantis will become but a faded memory, a pale imitation to be laughed at and forgotten." The Princess clasped her hands at the base of her throat, gleaming midnight eyes locking on Liria's face. "Are you ready, my shadow, to follow me on this path to greatness?"

It wasn't like she had any other choice, but Liria knew better than to say such things aloud. Instead, she bowed deeply, locking her gaze on the embroidered hem of Ione's gown. "Of course, your highness."

Princess Ione ran her slender fingers across the shimmering surface of Liria's wings, the sensation akin to hot knives slashing her wide open. Her breath caught in her throat, the urge to protest becoming the very thing that ensured her silence as the magical chains which bound her to her mistress snapped into full effect.

"Such flawless mystery in you, Liria. The subtlety of twilight, of hidden, magical things. You are well suited to accompany a jewel such as I." Another caress of Ione's fingers, her movements flicking away the long layers of trailing gauze that served to shield Liria's wings from view. "I wonder if Pharaoh Taos' wings are as magnificent as yours?"

"He's of the blood of Horus, your highness, and thus carries the wings of the falcon - whereas I am but a lowly fairy. I'm sure my wings are as nothing in comparison to the strong, feathered pinions of the angels."

"Hmmm. I suppose we shall see, soon enough." Ione tapped Liria's spine, silent permission for her to straighten. "I've heard the angels can even carry passengers, should the need arise."

So had Liria, but she didn't say as such, lest the Princess ask where she'd come across the knowledge. Instead, she adjusted the many layers of gauze which hung from her shoulders so that they once more protected her wings from casual view and said, "Perhaps, once you are wed, you can convince the Pharaoh to take you flying."

"Oh, yes." Ione clasped her hands to her full breasts, dark blue eyes shining. She blinked a few moments later, a crease forming between her brows. "And you will follow us, my shadow, will you not?"

Liria inclined her head again, glad of the way her hair swung forward to hide her face. "Such is my duty, your highness."

∼

Want to find out what happens next?
Grab your copy here:
The Heart of a Shadow

OTHER TALES BY SAMANTHA MARSHALL

Sorcery and Stardust

A sweeping science fiction series following the adventures of Arcana, Fenris, Caelum and Flare as they work to save time and space from the bestial warg and their vicious leader.

The Kin Chronicles

A paranormal romance series featuring the Kin, a race of people who can shift into animals and live alongside humanity in an alternate contemporary reality.

The Merged Worlds

A fantasy and paranormal romance series that starts in a time before our written history, when gods roamed the Earth, technology was crazily advanced and humanity shared their space with angels, vampires, fairies and a host of other magical creatures.

A Perfectly Paranormal Anthologies

A collection of paranormal romance anthologies in conjunction with several other wonderful authors.

To find out more about any of these, visit my website:

www.sliceofsammy.com

LOVE A FREE BOOK?

LEARN TO LET GO... OR BURN.

Dating Noah Acheson has always been gentle, predictable and above all, safe – but when the softly spoken foxkin breaks the rules of their carefully crafted relationship, Deanna cuts him off, retreating to her private sanctuary deep in the Australian bush.

Stinging from Deanna's rejection, Noah returns from a brief stint fighting fires in New South Wales to face an infinitely more vicious fire front in Victoria. Though his broken heart still very much belongs to Deanna Schellponte, he's determined not to chase her – until the wind changes, turning the fires towards pack land, and Deanna is reported missing.

With fire raging all around, Noah races into the bush to find the wolfkin he loves. To survive, Deanna and Noah must confront not only the fury of Mother Nature… but the ghost whose memory tore them apart.

Get your FREE copy here:
https://sliceofsammy.com/contact

WANT TO KEEP IN TOUCH?

I love to hear from, and hang out with, like minded people (yes, that's you!) and expand my tribe. Whilst I'm most active in my newsletter, you can also find me in other places from time to time! If you've already joined my mailing list and are still looking for more, then check out the following:

BLOG - www.sliceofsammy.com/blog

~

FACEBOOK - Samantha Marshall

~

INSTAGRAM - @sliceofsammy

~

TWITTER - @slice_of_sammy

Or send me an email at - samwrites@sliceofsammy.com - I love hearing from readers and authors alike!

See you there ^_^

Love,

Sammy
XOX

ABOUT THE AUTHOR

Hi, I'm Sam!

I've been writing my whole life, scribbling stories on anything close to hand – from the shopping list to napkins to post-it notes (don't mention post-its to hubby haha).

I grew up reading fantasy of the likes of Anne McCaffrey, Terry Pratchett, and their peers. I'm also a lifelong vampire fan, along with all things spooky. In my late teens I was introduced to paranormal romance and discovered a whole new layer of story-telling with a bit of a spicy edge! Taking what I learnt from all of the above, I devoted myself to creating full-bodied characters, meaty plots, epic adventure, and a little bit of naughty sauce on the side.

I completed a Diploma of Professional Writing and Editing after high school and spent the next several years in my writing cave, working on a novel that is now in a drawer somewhere, followed by a couple of others who shared the same fate. (What can I say? I'm a recovering perfectionist.)

I came close to debuting my novel career in 2009, then ended up pregnant and took some time off to have kids. I debuted for real in 2019 with *Sorcery and Stardust* and won ARRA's Favourite Debut Romance Author for 2019, which was extremely cool!

I write speculative fiction that is a fusion of multiple sub-genres and therefore doesn't fit particularly well into any of them, but after many years and a lot of angst, I'm okay with that. I love all my characters and their stories for different reasons, but have a soft spot for an excellent villain and a tortured protagonist.

I currently live in south east Melbourne, Victoria, with my hubby, two kids, a Golden Retriever and a turtle. I volunteer with the Romance Writers of Australia, and I'm passionate about great writing, interesting characters, chai tea and happily ever afters.

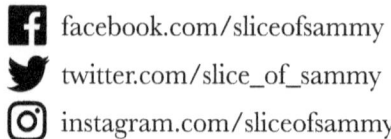

facebook.com/sliceofsammy

twitter.com/slice_of_sammy

instagram.com/sliceofsammy

www.ingramcontent.com/pod-product-compliance
Lightning Source LLC
Chambersburg PA
CBHW020011140726
47904CB00018B/2218

Contents